ON DECK FOR LOVE

REBECCA TALLEY

DUBON PUBLISHING

DuBon Publishing

CHAPTER ONE

When the knock sounded, Meg Summers glanced from her laptop screen to her watch. Was it time already? "Why did I let her talk me into this?" she muttered under her breath as she trudged to the front door of her sparsely decorated condo.

Shayla, her best friend since high school, stood there with a much too big smile and wide, excited eyes. "Do you have all your stuff?"

"I guess."

Shayla stepped inside, then brushed her naturally red curly hair off her shoulders. "It is one hot, humid day. Even for Houston." She fanned herself with her hand. "This is going to be the best vacation of all vacations. Ever."

While shaking her head, Meg shut the front door. Shayla had always been the perky, upbeat part of their duo. Sometimes it was more annoying than others. "If you say so."

Shayla pointed at Meg. With a serious expression she said, "You may not be Debbie Downer about this. I forbid it. We are going to have a blast."

"Because going on a singles cruise screams blast." Meg couldn't think of a worse way to spend the next week. All she could envision was a bunch of loser guys trying to hit on her. *Not what I want or need right now.*

"This is going to be super fun!" Shayla's green eyes danced.

Meg walked into the small kitchen and Shayla followed closely behind her. "I should've said no when you first brought up this crazy idea," Meg said, reaching for a glass. She filled it with some ice.

"It isn't crazy!" Shayla perched her hands on her hips. "People meet their significant others on cruises all the time."

"They do?" Meg gave her too-enthusiastic BFF a look of disbelief.

"Eighty-two percent of all those who go on singles cruises leave with the beginning of a relationship." Shayla said it with such conviction, Meg almost believed her. *Almost.*

"You just pulled that stat out of your—"

"I did not. It's totally true. And even if it isn't, why not take a chance?" Shayla grabbed the glass from Meg and added some water to it.

"For one, I have a ton of work to do if I want to launch my online business in less than three weeks." There was still so much to do before her website would be ready. Then there was all the social media marketing to schedule. And editing all the videos. She'd invested too much money to not meet her deadline.

Shayla waved her hand. "You can leave that for a week."

"Uh, uh. I'm taking my laptop with me and working. I need to upload my meal plans and exercise videos to my website, integrate the software so customers can sign up for my weight training program, and I have to test it to make sure there aren't any bugs." Shayla didn't understand all the work it entailed to get this business going. Sure, she was supportive, and had even encouraged Meg to pursue it last year when it was only a kernel of an idea, but there was a long list of tasks that had to be completed if Meg wanted this to be successful.

Shayla drew in a deep breath. "Meg!"

"What?"

"You promised you'd go on the cruise with a good attitude." Shayla wagged her finger at Meg.

Meg leaned back against the counter and crossed her arms in front of her chest. "No, no. I said I'd come because you said it was all you wanted for your birthday—your birthday wish—last month. I never agreed to have a good attitude about a bunch of weirdos who have no concept of a real relationship." A vision of some old, bald guy with a hairy back and leering eyes popped into her head and she shuddered.

"Okay. Then for my next birthday wish," Shayla raised her eyebrows, "I want you to be open to meeting someone."

"Uhh, that's blackmail." Meg wasn't about to be manipulated.

"Come on." Shayla gave a dramatic sigh. "You never know what might happen."

Meg stepped past Shayla and flopped on the couch. "Based alone on my last four first dates, I'm pretty sure I have an idea. Dating and relationships are totally overrated."

Shayla sat next to Meg. "Well, maybe your soul mate will be on this cruise."

Meg started laughing. "Actually, you're right."

"I am?" Shayla blinked.

Meg picked up her romance novel from the table and said, "Yep, here he is. I'll bring him with me. His name is Rolf."

Shayla threw her hands in the air. "I don't know what to do with you."

"Let me work while we're on the cruise. You go meet people and I work. Win-win." Seemed to make perfect sense to Meg.

"No way. You are going to be social. And you're going to like it." Shayla stood, then walked over to her bag and pulled something out. "And to make that happen, I bought you this."

"Bought me what?" Meg was afraid to ask.

Shayla held a blue dress in her hands. "Isn't it adorable? And you will be stunning. It'll totally bring out the blue in your eyes. And you can wear your hair up in a twist."

"Uhh, I'm not sure. It seems a little too much for me." Meg eyed it. "Make that a little too *little* for me." The dress would show way more of Meg than she wanted.

"You've worked so hard and for so long for your rockin' hot body, and you need to show it off."

It was true that Meg had transformed her body. Once she was a chubby kid with lots of extra padding and rolls. Now she had well-defined, lean muscles, and less than 18% body fat. Still, it was hard to ignore the nickname that still rang in her ears. *Megaton, Megaton, Megaton.* It had been coined by AJ, a rude, obnoxious boy she knew in middle school. It was hard to forget about all the body shaming she endured through the years for being overweight. "I don't know."

"My third birthday wish is that you wear this dress on the cruise and you like it. You'll look amazing. I promise." Shayla held the dress out to Meg.

Meg snatched it. Maybe Shayla was right. "Fine. But only because you're my bestie."

"Admit it. You think the dress is cute."

Meg held up the dress. "In an over-the-top kind of way, sure."

"You need to loosen up and have some fun." Shayla did some dance moves to an imaginary song.

Meg couldn't help but smile at Shayla's excitement. Maybe this cruise wouldn't be as bad as she thought. *Maybe.*

"You're all packed, right? Where are your bags?" Shayla glanced around the room.

"I'll get them."

"Well, get to it." Shayla tapped her wrist. "Time is wasting. And we need to be there early to board the ship."

"Galveston is a little over an hour from here. We have plenty of time." Meg grabbed her laptop so she could log out and shut it down.

"Nope. We want to be there so we can find the hottest men first."

Meg let out a long breath. They had plenty of time, but she knew

Shayla would continue to badger her, so she gave in and went back to her bedroom to get her suitcases. "I think we're leaving way too early. We can't even get on the boat until after two o'clock," she said while she rolled her suitcase into the living room.

"Better early than late." Shayla clapped her hands. "This is going to be so awesome."

Meg hefted her suitcase and a couple smaller bags into the back of Shayla's silver Toyota, then took her seat in the front.

Shayla blasted some music and they joined in the chorus of Katy Perry's "Firework" while they mounted the 45 Freeway headed south to Galveston. Over the music Shayla shouted, "Within a few hours, we might meet our Mr. Rights."

Meg was certain that if she met anyone, it'd be Mr. Wrong, but she didn't want to keep raining on Shayla's parade by saying it out loud. Humoring her BFF was a better choice. Besides, going on a singles cruise wouldn't kill her. She'd have plenty to eat, lots of sunshine, and if she was lucky, Shayla would meet someone and leave Meg alone to focus on her business.

"I THINK the shuttle will meet us over here," Shayla said, pointing to an area next to the parking lot.

Meg rolled her suitcase behind her. Perspiration formed around her hairline and at the back of her neck, making her wish she'd put her hair in a ponytail instead of leaving it down. Mid-July in southern Texas was typically hot and humid—emphasis on humid. She tried to fan herself with her hand once they reached the shuttle stop, but it didn't matter. "I'm planning to jump in the pool before we even get to our room."

"In your clothes?" Shayla said, crinkling her nose.

"Would it matter?" Meg pulled at her damp shirt and looked forward to some air conditioning on the shuttle bus.

They boarded the bus and headed down the street. As they

neared the pristine white, several-story ship, Meg was struck by how immense it was. "Wow, that is one big boat."

"Isn't it awesome? There's like eleven decks or something. And a couple of pools, a waterslide, a casino, restaurants, dance clubs. This is going to be the best ever." Shayla nodded and her hoop earrings swayed.

Despite her vow to not enjoy this cruise, Meg's excitement coursed through her. Maybe it would actually be fun to go on a cruise.

"Oh, did I tell you I saw Kirsten Shupe?" Shayla said as they walked into the check-in area.

Meg pulled her wallet out of her purse and fished her driver's license out of it. "Where did you see her?"

"I was coming out of Jimmy Choo at The Galleria."

"You and your shoe obsession."

"A girl can never have too many shoes." Shayla waved her hand. "Anyway, I almost walked right into Kirsten. I haven't seen her since high school."

Meg handed her ID to the Hispanic woman at the counter who looked it over, then tapped some keys on her computer.

"That's good, I guess." Kirsten Shupe was not someone Meg ever wanted to see again.

Shayla arched an eyebrow. "Don't tell me you still hate her."

Meg blew out a breath. The agony of being in class with Kirsten was still seared into her memory. "She was totally rude to me in our yearbook class."

The woman at the counter handed Meg back her ID. "Here is your cruise card. It will allow you to board the ship at the ports. Please hang onto it. You can now walk over there." The woman pointed to her left.

"Thank you," Meg said and collected her card. She started walking toward a long hallway tugging her suitcase behind her.

"I can't remember what Kirsten even did," Shayla said as she came up behind Meg.

"Oh, I remember it vividly." The memories heated Meg's cheeks. "It started when she read my copy for the theater department out loud and made fun of it. She told me I should never write anything, even a grocery list. Everyone thought she was so hilarious. Then she made snide remarks to me for the rest of the year."

"But that was a long time ago." Shayla shrugged. "I'm sure we've all changed since then."

"Some people never change. And Kirsten Shupe is one of them." Meg had plenty of proof to back up her claim.

"Are you going to carry your grudge against her forever?"

The way Shayla said it, it sounded foolish to still hang onto the memories, but Meg remembered how Kirsten made her feel. Why should she forget that? "Maybe."

CHAPTER TWO

Drew McDermott hoisted his suitcase from the shuttle bus, then handed his younger brother, Joey, the other suitcase.

Joey took it and said, "Aubrey wanted to go on a cruise."

Drew held up his hand. "No talking about your ex. This cruise is to help you forget all about her."

"I wanted to marry her. We talked about it and everything."

Joey sounded so defeated, and his brown eyes seemed so sad, but Drew was determined to help his brother meet someone new. "I know, but it's been three months since she married that dude. You have to move on, bro." Drew didn't want to be harsh with his brother, but Joey had wallowed long enough.

Joey let out a breath.

"This singles cruise will be a great way to meet other women." Drew had booked this cruise for the both of them a few months ago, then surprised Joey with it, hoping to get his younger brother out of the funk he was in.

Joey shrugged. "If you say so."

"We'll have a good time, you'll see." Drew had to do all in his power to make this cruise memorable and help Joey realize he could be happy with another woman.

"I don't know about that." Joey slouched.

Drew set his suitcase down and grabbed his brother by the shoulders. "Look, I know having your girlfriend run off with one of your college buddies was rough. But what's done is done. You have to let go of it and move forward."

Joey met Drew's gaze. "What about you?"

"This isn't about me." Drew wasn't going to let Joey turn this back on him.

"But you haven't had a girlfriend since college."

Drew shifted his weight. "I haven't had time. I've been busy building my career."

"Me too."

Drew gave Joey a skeptical look. If Drew didn't take the lead, Joey would mope around and end up not meeting anyone on this cruise. Even though Drew wasn't interested in a relationship with a woman right now—he didn't need, or want, any complications in his life—he had to do something, or Joey would spend all week sulking. "All right. I'll make you a deal. Are you game?"

"I guess."

"We'll both be open to meeting women on this cruise. And we'll both make an effort." He stuck out his hand. "You in?"

"Sure." Joey gave Drew's hand a weak shake.

Drew clapped Joey on the shoulder. "Let's go meet some women then."

As Meg and Shayla entered the boat, they were shuffled into the large theater to listen to safety procedures should there be any problems at sea. Meg gazed around. To her right was a group of men who were obviously friends. She assumed they were some frat pack coming to hook up with women. She spotted a large group of women who appeared to be college-aged. They were giggling and pushing each other. A few of them were waving at the guys from that group of men. *Typical. This is so not want I want to do.*

"Ooo, look at the guy over there?" Shayla inclined her head to her left. "He is so hot."

Meg scanned the crowd. "The one with the long beard?"

"No, the one wearing the white baseball hat."

"I guess." Meg felt much more like she was in a meat market than a cruise ship. Everyone seemed to be eyeing each other up and down to see who was the best specimen. It made Meg want to sprint out of there, but she couldn't. So, she told herself to suck it up to appease her best friend.

After the petite blond woman finished her speech on the safety aspects, she excused them to go find their staterooms.

Meg walked in front of Shayla, lugging her suitcase behind her. She turned to say something over her shoulder and didn't notice the crowd had stopped moving ahead of her. She felt the impact of running into someone and turned in enough time to step right on his foot. "I'm so sorry," she said, her face warming.

"No problem. I have another foot. I can hop on that one to get to my room." A man with thick dark hair and mesmerizing brown eyes said.

Meg forgot to breathe for a moment. She blinked, then cleared her throat. "I should've been paying better attention. I hope I didn't hurt your foot too much."

"I'm sure it'll be fine." He smiled and it made her heartbeat slip into her stomach.

"Again, I'm so sorry. I really am. I'm sorry. I'll try to . . . keep my foot out of the way of your foot . . . so that they don't . . . collide. Again. Because . . . that would, maybe, hurt your foot." *Please stop talking. Right now. Don't say another word.* "Yeah, so anyway. . . Uh . . . Sorry."

Someone squeezed between them, followed by several other

people, as everyone began to move out of the theater. Before she knew it, he was gone in a sea of strangers.

When Shayla caught up with Meg near the elevator, she said, "What were you saying to that devastatingly handsome guy in front of us?"

"I was making a fool out of myself." Meg wished she could call back all the nonsensical things she'd said to him. "I babbled some kind of apology."

"For staring at his gorgeousness?" Shayla said with wide eyes.

Meg shook her head. "No. I stepped on his foot in that crowd. And then I over apologized because, for some reason, my mouth wasn't working right."

Shayla giggled.

"What?" Meg gave her a sharp look. They walked into the elevator and Meg pushed the button next to the number two.

"It's called love at first sight." Shayla said it in a sing-songy voice.

"Hardly." Meg rolled her eyes. "I was flustered because I'd stepped on his foot." Sounded like a plausible explanation. Much more plausible than she was instantly attracted to some man she'd never met before.

"Hopefully you'll see him again." Shayla smiled. "And maybe he'll have a hot friend for me."

Meg shrugged on the outside. On the inside, she was freaking out. She'd just met probably the most handsome man she'd ever seen. And what did she do? Stepped right on his foot and then sounded like a total imbecile who couldn't construct a decent sentence. *How embarrassing*. Of course, she reminded herself, it didn't matter. On a ship this size, she'd probably never see him again, and even if she did, she wasn't here to meet men like Shayla was. Meg was here to work, not get sidetracked by a man. Or get involved with a man. Any man. Even one that made her heart do somersaults.

Except a teeny, tiny, miniscule part of her fantasized what it might be like to be distracted by a man like that.

"Meg? Meg? Meeeeggg?" Shayla said.

"What?" Why was Shayla acting so impatient?

"I've been trying to get your attention but you were somewhere else." Shayla elbowed her. "You were thinking about that guy."

"Uh, no," she lied. Shayla did not need to think Meg was at all interested in him. Or any other man on the boat. If Shayla even had an inkling that Meg thought he was attractive, she'd be relentless. "I was thinking I should change the colors on my website. Maybe stick with neutral colors, like beige with some brown details. Yes, a chocolate brown would be a better color." Like the inviting brown depths of that man's eyes. *Stop it! Get a hold of yourself.*

The elevator doors opened to deck two. "This is where our room is," Shayla said.

They walked down the hallway until they found room 2307.

Shayla grinned. "This is going to be so fantastical."

"That isn't even a word," Meg said, trying to reign in Shayla's enthusiasm.

"Sure it is. It's a cross between fantastic and magical. Fantastical." She laughed.

Meg rolled her eyes.

Inside the brightly colored room, Meg hung up a few items in the small closet, then put her suitcase at the bottom.

"What should we do now?" Shayla flopped on the bed. "We have a little while before dinner. Our assigned table is in The Reef restaurant."

Meg grabbed her laptop, but Shayla stood quickly and took it from her. "No work tonight."

"But—"

Shayla pointed at Meg. "Tonight is about loosening up and enjoying ourselves. We are going to mingle and meet men."

"I need—"

Shayla held up four fingers and wiggled them. "For my fourth birthday wish, I want you to forget about work, and everything else, and meet men."

Meg drew in a breath. "Exactly how many birthday wishes do you think you get?"

"Twenty-eight. That's the rule." Shayla set the laptop on the bed, just out of Meg's reach. "You get as many birthday wishes as your age."

Meg placed her hands on her hips. "Who made that rule?"

"The birthday gods." Shayla gave Meg an incredulous look. "Everyone knows this rule."

Meg rubbed her temples. "I feel like this birthday wish thing is going to haunt me during the whole cruise."

Shayla looped her arm through Meg's. "My dear Meg, this cruise is all about meeting men and having a good time. You agreed to celebrate my birthday here with me. On this cruise. It follows that you would do what I want to do. Right?" Shayla patted Meg's hand. "So, dinner?"

Knowing she was beat, Meg said. "Fine. I'll go do dinner."

"And the mix and mingle."

An image of the man with the magnetic brown eyes flashed through her mind, but she shooed it out. "Okay. And the mix and mingle thing. But tomorrow you have to let me do some work or I'll never make my launch deadline. I have all sorts of social media scheduled, and that I've paid for, and if I don't have a website to launch that will be a problem."

"All right, all right. You can have some work time tomorrow." Shayla held up her hand. "Promise. But tonight, we have fun."

Shayla stepped over to her closet and pulled out a flowery dress. "Wear this."

"Why? I have plenty of clothes to wear." Shayla could be annoying at times, especially when it came to Meg's wardrobe.

"I know. And they're *kinda* cute. But you'll look irresistible in this." Shayla held the dress out to Meg.

"You already gave me that blue one."

"That's for one of the special, dressy nights. I think it's called the captains dinner or something. I brought this one for you to wear for our first night." Shayla held the dress up to Meg.

"You think I can't dress myself?" It was true that Meg's style wasn't as showy as Shayla's, but it wasn't like she dressed like a grandma or something.

"I think you can dress yourself."

Meg gave Shayla a questioning look.

"You need a little help to add some flair to your wardrobe. That's all."

"I give up." Meg took the dress from Shayla.

Drew and Joey followed the crowd toward the elevators after being shuffled out of the theater where they'd learned about safety procedures.

"There are so many people here," Joey said, gazing around.

"A whole boatload of single women. Maybe you could meet that blond woman who gave the safety presentation. She was pretty cute."

"Not my type," Joey said.

The elevator doors opened and they stepped inside. As they rode the elevator, Drew's thoughts shot back to the woman with stunning blue eyes and silky, long dark hair. His gaze was immediately drawn to her full lips as she tried to apologize for stepping on his foot. He had to smile at the way she stumbled over her words. Without warning, and before he could ask her name, he was swallowed up in the crowd. He tried to keep his eyes on her, but she disappeared somewhere behind him.

They exited the elevator and walked down the long hall toward their stateroom. Drew opened the door and stepped inside.

"Hey," Joey said, pulling Drew from his thoughts of the mysterious, tongue-tied, foot-stomping woman.

"Huh?"

"Which bed do you want?" Joey brushed past him.

Drew shrugged. "I don't care."

Joey planted himself on the bed to their left. "I'll take this one then."

"Whatever."

"What's with you?" Joey asked, studying Drew with a discerning look.

"Nothing." Drew wasn't about to tell his brother that a woman had already caught his attention. This cruise was about Joey, not him. And sure, he'd made a deal with his brother, but honestly, Drew didn't have time for a woman. His last relationship ended because he never spent time with . . . her. He couldn't remember much about his last relationship, which was reason enough not to get involved. An image of the woman popped into his head again.

"Why are you smiling?"

Drew wiped at his mouth. "I'm not."

Joey perched on the edge of the bed. "You seem preoccupied or something."

"Nah. Let's get settled, then go up to the deck with the pool. I think we can get something to eat there." Food would certainly distract him from thoughts of the beautiful woman.

CHAPTER
THREE

With her trademark I'm-trying-not-to-get-irritated way, Shayla said, "Are you ready to go? You're taking forever."

Unruffled, Meg finished brushing her hair then fashioned it into a messy bun.

"You should wear your hair down," Shayla said, sitting on the bed. She adjusted the straps on her wedges.

"Why?" Meg wasn't there to impress anyone, and her hairstyle proved it.

"Because it's so long and luxurious. All us mere mortals would kill for hair like yours."

Meg waved her hand to dismiss the compliment.

"I know what you're doing." Shayla fluffed her hair, then stood.

Meg looked at herself in the mirror, ignoring the insinuation.

"You're trying to be unattractive to repel the men."

"That's ridiculous. What woman tries to be unattractive?" Meg hated that Shayla read her so well.

"It won't work, you know." Shayla applied some lip gloss. "You're still beautiful."

Meg shrugged a shoulder in reply.

Shayla raised her eyebrows and looked directly at Meg. "Birthday wish, remember?"

Meg closed her eyes and pinched the bridge of her nose. She could fight Shayla all week or give in and play along. She opened her eyes. "Fine." She let down her hair, shook her head a few times, then flashed her biggest smile. "Better?"

"Much." Shayla gave Meg some perfume. "You can wear this."

Meg didn't want to argue, so she spritzed her neck with the light, floral scent.

Shayla opened the door. "Let's go walk around the deck and see who we can meet."

After taking the elevator from the second floor up to the Lido Deck, they walked over to the pool. People were already sitting on the lounge chairs and talking. A warm breeze laced with salty, sea air fanned Meg's face.

"Looks like we can get a drink over there." Shayla pointed toward The Red Iguana Cantina.

Meg followed Shayla to a counter. While standing in line, Shayla whispered, "Hot guy alert. Over there." She inclined her head to the left.

There were at least five men in that vicinity. "Which one?"

"Tall, blond hair, red t-shirt, huge biceps."

"Oh, yeah. I see him." He was semi-attractive, but not Meg's type. Meg wasn't sure if her type existed except in the romance novels she read.

"Let's go talk to him." Shayla smiled.

"Sure." If Shayla met someone right away, she'd leave Meg alone to work.

They made their way over to the guy, who grinned when he saw them approaching.

"Hi. My name is Shayla and this is Meg."

"Nice to meet you. My name is Greg. Would you like to join me for some drinks?" His smile exposed crooked teeth.

"That sounds great," Shayla said in her sweetest voice.

Shayla and Greg started talking while Meg's gaze roamed the deck. It wasn't that she was specifically looking for the man she'd seen earlier—the one she'd stepped on—but if she happened to see him, she wouldn't look away.

A guy with too-short shorts, too-much chest hair peeking out of his polo shirt, and wearing a gold chain sat at the table. He spoke in an accent Meg couldn't place. "Hello."

"Hi." She wasn't at all interested in this guy. He must've bathed in the cheapest cologne money could buy.

"My name is Eduardo." He leaned in. "I don't suppose you have a map?"

Meg gave him a confused look. "Uh, no. Why?"

"Because I keep getting lost in your eyes."

Seriously? He just said that? I wanna throw up. Meg gave him a courtesy laugh.

With a leer, he said, "Would you like to go dancing with me tonight?"

I'd rather sacrifice myself to a starving tiger. "Actually, I'm not a dancer. At all."

He ogled her, making her skin feel like it had spiders running all over it. "We could spend the night doing something else." He licked his lips and smirked. She resisted the urge to slap that slimy smile off his face.

Pulling her phone from her pocket, Meg said, "I'm so sorry, but I have to answer this." She pretended to answer her phone. "Oh, yeah. I'll be there in a second." She looked at the smarmy man and said, "Nice to meet you, but I have to go."

She stood quickly and tapped Shayla on the shoulder. "I'll meet you later." With that, she left.

This cruise was starting out *exactly* as she'd thought. A bunch of loser men trying to score. They'd barely left the dock and she already wanted to throw herself overboard. This week was going to feel more like a month. Maybe even a year.

She walked along the deck and gazed out over the ocean. An idea for her website popped into her head, and she rushed to the elevators. She went down to the second floor and hurried into her room. Inside, she pulled out her laptop and began writing some copy that she wanted to include on her website, 4FHealth.com. She wanted to incorporate her tagline: Food + Fitness + Fun = Fabulous. She played with a few color variations and the placement of some of the photos, then reread her copy.

The door flung open and Meg's head popped up.

"There you are," Shayla said. "You totally disappeared on me."

"I didn't think you'd notice with Mr. Muscles."

"Yeah, he couldn't stop talking about the weight he can lift. Boring." Shayla shook her head. "Never even asked anything about me. He went on and on and on about himself. But I met this other guy, Sean. He seemed pretty nice, but he wasn't very cute. His face seemed too small for his head."

"Sounds like you're making the rounds." Nothing about that was at all appealing to Meg.

"You're supposed to be up there with me. Not down here on your computer. Remember?" Shayla frowned.

"I had this idea and had to come down here to write it down before I forgot." It was true. It also happened to be the perfect excuse to hide out in the room and avoid any and all social activities.

"Come on, Meg. You promised." Shayla put her hand on her hip. She tapped her phone screen then showed it to Meg. "See what time it is?"

"Yeah."

"That means it's dinner time and we are supposed to be in The Reef Restaurant for our seating. Right now." Shayla gave Meg an expectant look.

"Can I finish this?" Meg only needed a few minutes to proofread her work and save it.

"I guess." Shayla sat on the bed and tapped her fingernails on the side table.

Meg stared at her. "Do you have to do that?"

"Oh, sorry." Shayla patted her thighs instead.

After several tappity-tap-taps, Meg said, "Not any better. I can still hear you."

Shayla stood. "Are you almost done?"

Meg pushed out a strong breath. "I can see you aren't going to let me finish this."

"Okay, good. Let's go."

Meg shut her laptop, then followed Shayla down the hall to the elevators. They rode up to the seventh floor where their dining assignment was.

"Looks like a nice restaurant," Shayla said over her shoulder as the short Asian hostess lead them to their table.

Meg hoped there would be delicious food and no weird guys at their table. She wanted to enjoy a nice meal without any awkward conversation.

The hostess took them to a large circular table near the windows. *At least I'll have a nice view.*

Five men and three other women filled the seats, leaving two for Meg and Shayla.

"Hi, I'm Shayla and this is my best friend, Meg."

Meg gave a small wave, then sat next to Shayla.

Everyone took turns introducing themselves. Meg sat next to a guy with a shaved head and a tattoo on his neck under his left ear. She didn't want to stare, but the tattoo looked a bit ominous with a snake and a sword.

"Name's Dwayne," he said with a deep voice.

"Hi." Meg wasn't sure what else to say.

"I'm from San Antonio. You?" He sat back.

"I live in Houston." Small talk was always the worst.

"This is my third cruise. Good place to hook-up. Know what I mean?" He eyed her up and down, then sat up and sipped his drink.

If I yelled fire would I be arrested on the spot and sent to jail? Because that'd be better than sitting next to this loser tonight.

"We can get together after dinner." He moved in closer to her, the stench of alcohol on his breath.

Meg swallowed back the bile that rose up her throat, then said, "Sorry, we've already signed up for an activity.

"I don't mind doing that first." He took another sip of his drink.

Meg elbowed Shayla.

"Ow," Shayla said.

Meg turned to her and made big eyes, then mouthed, "Help."

Shayla leaned across Meg and said to Dwayne, "You'll have to excuse my friend, she hasn't been herself since her outbreak."

"Outbreak?" He wrinkled his nose.

"Very contagious skin fungus. You probably don't want to get too close to her." Shayla made a face, and Meg bit her lip to keep from smiling.

"Oh. Yeah." Dwayne scooted away.

Meg stood and said, "Excuse me. I need to use the restroom." She scurried out of the dining room as quickly as possible.

Inside the dimly lit restroom, she tried to convince herself to go back out there, but all she could think about was escaping, even if that meant diving into shark-infested waters and swimming back to Galveston. She stared at herself in the mirror. *Why, oh why, did I ever listen to Shayla. She is so fired as my BFF.*

The door opened. "There you are," Shayla said. "Come back to dinner."

"Are you kidding me? With that Dwayne guy? No way. I'd rather give up eating for the rest of my life. Even longer." A shudder of disgust raced down her back.

"We don't have to go back to the dining room. We could go to one of the other places to eat," Shayla offered.

Meg let out a breath. She didn't want to completely discount going back if Shayla was set on it. "Well, did you see any interesting men at our table?"

"Ew, no." Shayla made a face. "Let's go somewhere else and see if the choices are better."

Meg relaxed, then laughed. "Thank you. I was afraid you'd drag me back in there."

They left the small bathroom and took an elevator to the Lido Deck. Several places to eat surrounded a large pool.

"Looks like we can get a taco bar there," Shayla pointed. "Or pizza over here."

"And seafood across the deck," Meg said.

"I think I'd like a taco salad." Shayla turned toward the taco bar.

"Sounds good."

After getting their salads, they found a table and sat. A din of conversation floated above them. Men and women of all shapes and sizes milled about the deck. Some laughed, others obviously flirted, while others seemed to be deep in conversation.

Meg took a bite of her salad. She sat back, then noticed the guy whose foot she'd stepped on was standing in a small group with another guy and three women. Meg swallowed hard and tried to avert her eyes.

Shayla immediately noticed. "What?" Shayla glanced around. "Ohh, that guy is super attractive."

"I know."

"You've seen him?" Shayla studied her with eager eyes.

"Uh, yeah. That's the guy whose foot I stepped on." The memory sent a rush of heat across Meg's cheeks.

Shayla giggled. "That guy with the light brown hair in the blue shirt?"

"No, the taller one standing next to him." She'd notice his good looks even if he were seated across the Astro's baseball field at Minute Maid Park.

"Oh. Well, he's cute too." Shayla smiled in their direction.

"Stop." Meg scooted away from Shayla and covered her face with her hand.

"What?"

Meg positioned herself so her backside faced the men. "Don't get their attention."

"Why not? They're some of the most attractive men on this ship." Shayla kept gazing in their direction.

"Because. I'm way too embarrassed to see him again."

"Come on." Shayla shrugged. "It was an accident. You stepped on his foot. So not a big deal."

"Not to you." Meg kept her head down.

Shayla waved her hand. "As usual, you're making a big thing out of nothing."

"Hey, I resent that." Meg never made a big deal out of anything. Ever. She didn't know what Shayla meant by that remark. Stepping on that guy's foot was akin to going to a job interview only to find out afterwards that you had a big booger hanging out of your nose. Didn't Shayla understand that? She acted like it was nothing at all.

Shayla perched on the edge of her chair and even more obviously stared in their direction. "Sorry. I just want to meet that guy."

AFTER THE GROUP of women they were talking to moved on, Drew sidled up next to his brother. "Did you like any of those women?"

Joey shook his head.

Drew wanted to encourage Joey to find someone to take his mind off Aubrey, but Joey was making that impossible. "Have you seen any interesting women yet?"

Joey shifted his weight. "I don't know."

"What about that blond over there?" Drew slyly glanced in the direction of a woman in black shorts.

Joey shrugged. He glanced around the Lido Deck. "That one over there is cute." He tilted his head to the right.

Drew scanned the area to see which one Joey was referring to and when his gaze settled on two women at a table, he smiled. It was the woman who'd stepped on his foot. "You mean at that table?" Drew pointed indiscreetly.

Joey nodded.

"Which one?" It would be awkward if Joey was attracted to Toe-Stomper. Not that Drew was attracted to her. Well, maybe he was. A little. Okay, maybe more than a little.

"The one with red hair."

Drew let out a small puff of breath. "What about the brunette?" *With the amazing eyes and beautiful smile.*

"You know I'm not into brunettes anymore."

Drew nodded. A redhead might be exactly what Joey needed. "Go over and talk to her."

Joey kicked at the ground.

"Look, man, we're here for you to get back in the game."

"See, that's the thing." Joey held out his hand. "I don't really want to be *in the game*."

"I brought you here to meet women so you can stop moping." Drew wanted to be patient with his brother, but enough time had passed, and Joey needed to move on with his life.

Joey glanced around. "I know. I don't think I'll ever meet anyone as awesome as Aubrey."

"You won't know that unless you try. Right?" Drew was certain Joey would find another woman to love, though he wasn't so sure he'd ever find that himself.

Joey scratched his head. "If you say so."

"Let's go over there." Drew started to walk toward the two women.

MEG TOOK another bite of her salad. At least the food was good, even if the men they'd met so far ranked lower than the creeper that lived down the street from her condo. He always seemed to stare at her with an unnerving expression when she passed him. She shuddered.

"There's a good-looking guy over there. The one with a beard." Shayla gave a jerk of her chin.

Meg sipped her water. "You should go talk to him."

"I meant for you." Shayla sat back in her chair.

"You don't need to find me a man." Shayla seemed to be on a crusade, but she needed to focus on finding herself a man, because Meg didn't need or want one.

"If I don't, you won't," Shayla said.

"I'm here on this singles cruise, aren't I?" What else did Shayla want from her?

With an arched eyebrow, Shayla said, "Against your will."

"No." She pointed at Shayla with her fork. "Not against my will."

Shayla leaned in. "Please, try to enjoy yourself."

"I told you I will." She shoved another bite into her mouth, the spicy salsa tingling on her tongue.

"Excuse me, ladies," a deep voice behind them said.

Meg twisted to see who it was and as soon as her gaze met his, her heart squeezed tight. *The guy that I stepped on.*

"Hi," Shayla said enthusiastically.

"I'm Drew and this is my brother, Joey."

"Nice to meet you," Shayla said in her trademark flirty voice. "This is Meg and I'm Shayla."

"We've already met," Drew said, gesturing to Meg.

Meg nodded, her cheeks warm. "Yes. We kind of met."

Shayla started laughing. "Because you're the guy she plowed into?"

"Yes, yes I am." He smiled and it made Meg's stomach flip-flop.

"Do you want to sit down and join us?" Shayla asked.

"Sure." Drew sat in a chair next to Meg. "Nice to *officially* meet you."

"You too." This guy was handsome enough to make her swoon. She could lose herself in his eyes for days. Make that weeks.

Joey sat next to Shayla and they began a conversation.

"Do you make it a habit of stepping on men's toes?" He smiled and the skin around his dark chocolate eyes crinkled.

"Uh, not usually." Meg cleared her throat. "I really am sorry about that. I hope your foot is okay."

"I think it'll be fine," he said in a voice that was smooth and deep.

Meg pushed her plate away from her.

"We didn't mean to interrupt your dinner," he said in an apologetic tone.

"I was done." Meg's stomach was too quivery to allow her to eat anything else. Why was this guy having such an effect on her?

He leaned back in his chair and smiled. "We ate at the buffet."

"How was the smile?" *Oh no! Did I just say smile? Kill me now.*

"Smile?" His grin grew wide.

Meg wanted to crawl under the table. She sucked in a breath and said, "I meant food. How was the *food*?" This guy made her into a babbling idiot.

"Delicious."

Hoping to sound like a normal human, she said, "We tried the dining room, but that didn't work out very well." An image of the Dwayne dude flashed in her mind and gave her a shudder.

"The food wasn't good?"

She raised her eyebrows. "We didn't actually stay long enough."

"Ah, I see." He nodded. "Was it the company at the table?"

Meg let out a laugh. "I don't know about you, but I'm not really into this singles cruise scene."

"You're not?" He almost sounded surprised. Was that good or bad?

Meg shook her head. She hoped he wasn't into it either, but if he was, this conversation would be very short. "I came with Shayla to celebrate her birthday. We've been friends since high school and she's always wanted to go on a cruise."

"And you're the dutiful friend who came along to support her?"

Meg nodded. "Something like that."

"I'm here with my younger brother."

Meg glanced at Shayla and Joey who were both animated as they spoke. "They seem to be hitting it off."

"They do." Drew wore a smile that seemed satisfied. "Tell me about yourself, Meg, who isn't interested in a singles cruise."

She winced. "I guess I sounded a little harsh?"

Drew shrugged, then smiled.

She wanted to make it clear she wasn't here to have some shipboard one-night stand. "This kind of thing seems like such a meat market. Everyone is out for a fling."

"And you aren't into that?" Again, he seemed surprised. This man intrigued her.

"No." She studied him. "Are you?"

"If I said I wasn't, would you believe me?"

She arched an eyebrow. "I'm not sure."

He grinned. "I guess I have my work cut out for me."

What does he mean by that?

"Joey and I are thinking about checking out the karaoke lounge later," Shayla said, interrupting their conversation.

"I thought you wanted to do the activity on deck?" Meg said, still trying to figure out Drew.

Shayla turned to Joey. "Let's do that first?"

"Yeah. What do you say, bro?" Joey said to Drew.

"Sure. Sounds like the activity and the karaoke lounge would be great." He gazed at Meg with his hypnotic eyes. "What about you?"

Meg smoothed her hair. She didn't want to seem too eager to spend the evening with him. "Okay," she said casually.

They stood and walked over to the area behind the pool where a crowd was already congregating. When they stopped, a raven-haired woman with voluptuous assets turned to Drew. "Well, hello there. I'm Rhianna." She swung her arm around him. Meg tried to tamp down the flare of jealousy. After all, she'd only met this man and he was free to flirt with whomever he pleased.

"Hi, Rhianna. Nice to meet you." He turned toward Meg. "This is Meg."

Rhianna unwrapped her arm. "Oh. Sorry, honey. Didn't know he was taken already. You're a fast worker."

Taken? Fast worker? Hardly. A derisive laugh fell from Meg's mouth.

"I hope you enjoy your cruise," Drew said to the woman. He moved closer to Meg.

"Welcome to our Get-To-Know-You Activity here on the Lido Deck," a tall guy with short-cropped black hair said. "I am Matteo, your cruise director. My job is to make sure you have the best time of your life on this cruise." He fanned his arm out. "This is my crew and we're here to help you." He went on to introduce his crew of three women and another man. "Let's get started."

The crowd clapped and a guy in the back whistled.

"I want you to turn to your right and kiss that person." He let out a loud laugh. "Just kidding. Actually, turn to the people on either side of you and introduce yourself."

"Hi, I'm Drew. You are?" He looked at Meg and smiled.

"My name is Meg. Nice to meet you, Drew." She stuck out her hand.

"Very nice to meet you." He took her hand in his and a sizzle of energy ran up her arm. When their gazes locked, her heartbeat tripled. *What is happening?*

Without warning, Meg felt someone grab her around the waist and twirl her around. "Hello, my name is Alonso. I live in Louisiana and I'd like to get to know you." He planted a kiss on Meg's lips.

Drew pushed him off before Meg could react. "That's no way to treat a lady."

"Hey, man, I'm only doing what the director said." He raised his hands as if innocent of any wrong-doing. "Didn't know she was with you."

Drew stepped back and Alonso disappeared into the crowd. "On behalf of decent men, I'd like to apologize," Drew said.

Meg wiped her mouth and wished she had some Germ-X to gargle with. "Thanks."

"I don't know what got into that guy."

"Seems to be the vibe of this singles cruise." Meg grimaced.

"How about we go sit down somewhere?" He looked at her. "Unless you want to meet some more guys like that," he said in a teasing manner.

"I'll pass." Meg wanted to unmeet, unsee, and definitely unkiss all the men she'd run into so far—except for one.

They walked inside and found a table next to the window.

Meg looked at Drew. "If a singles cruise isn't your thing, why did you come?" She was eager to hear his answer.

"Joey was about to propose to this woman he'd been dating for over a year. The day before he planned to ask her, she told him she had fallen in love with one of their mutual friends and they were getting married."

Meg covered her mouth. "A friend did that to your brother? Wow. Must've hit him pretty hard."

"Yeah, he was devastated. He found out about six months ago, and he's been brooding about it ever since. I told him he needed to snap out of it and meet someone new. Then I booked this cruise for the both of us."

"You're a nice brother." She still wanted to know how he felt about being on the cruise with all these available women. "There are lots of single women here. For him. And for you."

He gave her a quick glance. "This cruise is for him. Not me."

"Because you aren't single?" It sounded like she was prying. Because, well, she was.

He laughed. "Oh, I'm very single. Have been for quite a while."

"Is that so?" Why would such a good-looking guy be single? And for quite a while.

"It's a long story."

Meg leaned in and rested her elbows on the table. "I love long stories."

"How about I give you the short version?" He leaned in toward her and she could feel the electricity pass between them.

"I'd like that." She couldn't wait to hear what he'd say.

"My parents are very driven. My father has his own law practice and my mother is a motivational speaker. They're a power couple." He paused and glanced out the window for a moment. "They wanted me to marry the daughter of one of my dad's colleagues."

"And that was bad?" Meg found herself fascinated by this story. And by this man.

"Candace was beautiful. Poised. Well-educated. A perfect match for an up-and-coming attorney like me. That's what my parents kept telling me anyway." Drew cleared his throat, then lowered his voice. "Drew, my boy, this is the woman for you. It doesn't matter if you love her or not. Marriage isn't about love. It's about prestige and social success." Drew leaned back.

"Wow. Your dad said that?" Sounded like his father was a harsh man.

"He'd always been hard on me. Even from elementary school he expected me to excel at everything. He told me that second was not good enough. I had to be first or I was a loser. He was pretty hard-core." A sad expression flashed across his face.

"That must've been difficult growing up." She wanted to touch his hand to comfort him, but she resisted.

Drew shrugged. "Candace and I dated for several months before we both realized we didn't want to marry each other. It took another few to break-up so our parents wouldn't be so mad. Since then, I've steered clear of relationships and focused on building my career."

"As an attorney?" She wanted to know as many details about this man as possible.

"Yes."

Meg peered at him. "And you like being a lawyer?"

Drew let out a long breath, then laced his fingers and put his hands behind his head. After a few moments, he said, "If I had it to do over again, I wouldn't have chosen this career." He leaned forward. "My dad pressured me into it. As in, he pretty much said if I didn't follow in his footsteps, he'd disown me."

"Pretty intense." Meg couldn't imagine being in that position.

"That's a good word for both my parents. Intense."

"What would you have chosen to do?" She was almost breathless as she waited for his response.

After a minute or so, he said, "My dream would be . . . Nah, it'll sound ridiculous." He glanced at her as if waiting for her to prod him on.

"No way. Dreams are never ridiculous. Eleanor Roosevelt said, 'The future belongs to those who believe in the beauty of their dreams.' I've repeated that to myself at least a million times," she said with as much encouragement as she could.

"Great quote." He nodded. "Sounds like you have some dreams too."

"I do."

He peered at her. "How about you share them?"

"Maybe I will." She smiled. "After you share yours." She hadn't been this interested in listening to a man in, well, a long time—a very long time.

He fumbled with the napkin dispense, then drummed his fingers on the table. Finally, he said, "I'd like to be a chef. Open my own restaurant."

"Really?" She hadn't expected him to say he wanted to be a chef. She wasn't sure what she expected, but that wasn't it.

He sat back. "See, it sounds foolish."

Worried that her expression had betrayed her surprise, she rushed to say, "Not at all. Owning your own restaurant and being a chef sounds awesome."

With a look of satisfaction, he said, "I've developed some of my own recipes."

Her eyes grew wide. "Seriously?" What else could this guy say?

He nodded. "I started cooking in college when I moved out on my own and was hooked. Started experimenting with different dishes and ingredients. I even took a couple culinary classes, but had to do it secretly."

“Why?” Meg had never met anyone like Drew.

“My dad is old school. Cooking isn’t very masculine. You know, women cook. Men don’t.” He cleared his throat. “No son of mine is going to spend his time in the kitchen. That’s women’s work.”

Meg had to laugh at the way Drew portrayed his father. “I’m sure he isn’t that bad.”

Drew raised his eyebrows.

“Have you cooked for anyone before?”

He shook his head. “Nope.”

“Why not?” If he loved to cook, she had to wonder why he hadn’t shared it with anyone before.

“Fear of rejection, I suppose.” He blew out a breath. “As long as I keep my cooking to myself, I can think about someday being a chef and owning a restaurant. Once it’s out there, I either have to change my life drastically and take a risk, or give up on my dream. I know that probably doesn’t make much sense.”

“It makes total sense to me.” She’d often felt the same way before making the plunge into her own fitness business. “If you ever need a taste tester, I volunteer.” The words tumbled out of her mouth before she could stop them. Now he was going to think she wanted to see him after this cruise. Which she didn’t. Or did she?

“I may take you up on that.” He smiled and it grabbed at her stomach. Somehow, he reminded her of someone, but she couldn't put her finger on it.

"Hey, what are you guys doing?" Shayla asked from behind, interrupting their intimate conversation. She sat in a chair next to Meg.

"Talking.” Meg scooted back from the table and turned toward her BFF. “Are you done with the get-to-know you stuff?"

Joey sat on the other side of Shayla. "We decided we were done. Too many weirdos."

"Has it occurred to you that there are some very strange people on this ship?" Shayla asked Meg.

Meg rolled her eyes. Besides Drew, all the men she'd met were nothing but bizarre.

"This one guy came up and started kissing her," Joey pointed at Shayla. "I wanted to teach him some manners."

"Was his name Alonso?" Meg asked, recalling the slimy guy who assaulted her with his lips.

"Yeah " Shayla made a face like she was nauseated.

"Kissed me too." A shudder ran up Meg's back.

"So ew." Shayla wiped at her mouth.

"I thought you were enjoying the games." Drew snickered. "Did you happen to meet Rhianna?"

Joey scratched his head. "No."

"Be grateful. Mother would not approve."

Joey and Drew started laughing.

Shayla looked over at Meg, who shrugged.

"Should we go check out the karaoke bar?" Shayla asked.

Meg didn't want to encourage her, so she said nothing. Singing, dancing, or anything related to performing in front of a crowd wasn't her favorite thing.

"Drew and I have been known to do a little karaoke in our time," Joey said. "Like at Shaun's wedding."

Drew shook his head.

"This sounds like an interesting story," Shayla said.

"Yeah, tell us what happened." Meg glanced between the two brothers.

"Suffice it to say, our cousin, Shaun, nor anyone else we know, has ever asked us to sing again." Drew shrugged.

"He said we sounded like, what was it?" Joey tapped his forehead.

"Moose during mating season," Drew said. "But we had a great time. Right, bro?"

Drew and Joey pounded each other's knuckles. "They didn't recognize our talent," Joey said.

"Moose? During mating season?" Meg started laughing.

"Everyone knows karaoke isn't about talent, it's about entertainment," Shayla said.

"We were definitely entertaining that night," Joey said.

Shayla clasped her hands together. "I know, I know, let's do a group performance. It'll be epic."

"Uh, uh." Meg held her hands up. "No way."

"Oh, come on. Remember when we did that dance for our talent show in high school?"

"Uh, yeah. The memory is seared into my brain, and that's why I refuse to let you rope me into something like that again." Meg knew much better than to trust Shayla when it came to performing. Shayla was a little crazy and way too eager to take risks.

"I still think our modern, interpretive dance to that Britney song was a-mazing." Shayla started singing, "Oops! . . I Did It Again."

"I think I'd use another word to describe it. Especially because we weren't dancers. At all. I still don't know why I let you talk me into it." Meg wanted to forget that performance ever took place.

"Because you love me. And it was fun."

"Was it?" Meg wouldn't use the word fun to describe that experience. *Humiliating* was a much better word. Meg went from her Megaton nickname—a name she despised—to her new one, Britney Wannabe, which she hated equally as much. Sure, that was years ago —even a lifetime ago—but the memory still stung.

"Come on. It's about having a good time. Letting loose." Shayla made big eyes at Meg. "Please? I promise it won't be embarrassing. We're all adults now, so it'll be great. Please?"

Joey joined in and said, "Please?"

Then it was Drew's turn. "Please?"

"No. I'll watch you three do it. And cheer you on from the audience." She absolutely did not want to get up on any stage.

In unison, they all said, "Please."

Meg looked at them with their cheesy smiles. "You're ganging up on me."

"Is it working?" Shayla asked. "We'll do something super easy. This is a cruise and it's all about enjoying ourselves."

"But I won't enjoy it." Meg didn't want to be a downer or look like she was no fun, but she also didn't want to humiliate herself again, especially in front of Drew. When she glanced at him with his encouraging expression, she softened. Maybe she was being too stiff and serious. "I'm going to regret this."

"That's a yes." Shayla threw her arms around Meg, then said, "What should we sing?"

"We could do 'She's Lost that Loving Feeling,'" Joey said.

"I hate it when she does that," Shayla said, then started laughing.

"*Top Gun* fan?" Joey asked.

"Oh yeah. It's a classic." If Shayla smiled any bigger her face would crack.

Drew said, "What about 'Bohemian Rhapsody?'"

"Seriously?" Meg gave him a quick look. "How would we ever lip synch to that song? It's so weird."

"You're probably right." Drew nodded.

"Let's do something from the 80s," Shayla said. "Or the 70s. Something upbeat."

Meg tried to think of a song. She needed to redeem herself, but also find an easy song. "I got it. YMCA."

They all looked at each other and shrugged.

"Okay, let's do that one," Shayla said. "We all know the moves, right? And we'll get the audience to do it with us. We'll be the coolest contestants of the night."

Even though Meg was out of her element, she felt a certain sense of satisfaction that she'd suggested the song. As they talked about it, went over the arm movements, and decided Joey would sing most of the song while the other three sang back up, she began to loosen up and almost enjoy the idea.

This cruise might not be so bad after all.

~

THEY ALL WALKED into the cozy lounge for the karaoke night. Tables and chairs surrounded a stage and a bar was situated toward the back. Dim lighting and deep red colors added to the ambience. Though Meg felt uncomfortable, the rest of the group's energy was contagious, and she figured she might as well join in. *Why not?*

A man and woman got up and sang some country song together. They weren't that bad as far as terrible singers went, which made Meg feel more confident about their number.

That couple was followed by three women who sang "Mean" by Taylor Swift. Meg couldn't help but reflect on her own life during the song and how she'd been hurt by other people. But, she reminded herself, she was stronger because of it and, like the girl in the song, she was living her life on her own terms now. She was on the cusp of launching a successful online business that would change the direction of her life.

Drew nudged her. "You seem to be deep in thought. Or do you just really like this song?"

Meg smiled at his perception. "I was thinking about my business."

"I don't think you've told me about it." He sounded genuinely interested.

"I'm certified as a personal trainer and I currently work as a nutritionist at Better Life, a wellness center in Houston, but I've been working on an online fitness and health website. 4FHealth.com. It stands for food plus fitness plus fun equals fabulous. I'm planning to launch it in three weeks. It'll be a subscription site with workouts, meal plans, motivational videos. I'm super excited."

"I hope you'll tell me all about it," Drew said. Meg was touched that he wanted to know more.

"Let's hear it for Shayla, Meg, Drew, and Joey," the enthusiastic DJ with black hair said. Meg turned to look at the DJ, who motioned for them to come forward. The audience gave them courtesy applause as they all strode up to the stage.

Meg instantly regretted her decision to perform. Every muscle in her body tensed as she looked out over the unfamiliar faces that all stared at her. *I can't do this.*

As if reading her thoughts, Drew leaned over and whispered, "You're going to do great. Let yourself feel the music and go with it."

When the music started, people began clapping to the beat. Meg's heart thudded against her ribs, but as the song continued, her body started to relax. She didn't sing too loudly, the other three had that covered. Then it came time to mark out the Y, M, C, then A. Meg was hesitant at first, but when she looked over at Drew and saw his encouraging smile, she put her hands above her head, let the music resonate through her body, and started jamming to the beat.

Through the next verse, she swiveled her hips, shook her shoulders and snapped her fingers while she tried to keep up with the words. *This performing thing isn't so bad after all. Actually, it's kinda fun.* She glanced at Shayla, who was really getting into the song. Joey and Drew were pointing at the audience, then shaking their hips. People were clapping and whistling.

The chorus started up again and Meg was ready to put her all into it. She threw her arms into the poses for Y, M, C, and A and shouted out the letters. The audience was singing along and Meg was feeling every note of the song.

She edged closer to the stage and during the last poses, she misjudged where she stood and stumbled. As she fell to the ground, her shoulder hit a table, knocking a drink over and splattering it across herself. She landed in a heap of arms and legs, liquid dripping down her forehead. There was an audible gasp and the music stopped.

Her face immediately lit on fire. Just as she was getting into this song and letting go of her inhibitions, she had to fall off the stage. And not simply fall, but her dress got twisted and exposed much more of herself than she wanted. There was little left to anyone's imagination.

Jumping to her feet, Meg ran from the room and kept running down the stairs. She didn't stop until she found her stateroom. She opened the door, slammed it behind her, then collapsed, face first, onto her bed. *I'm going to stay here for the rest of the cruise. I will not leave this room until we dock in Galveston.*

A few minutes later, the door flew open and Shayla said breathlessly, "Are you okay?"

Meg rolled over. "I'm fine." Physically, she had no injury, but her pride was critically—even mortally—wounded.

"I was so worried. It looked like you might have hurt yourself when you . . ."

"Say it! When I *fell*. Right. Off. The. Stage. Like the biggest klutz in the entire world." She wished the floor had opened up and swallowed her right there in that lounge.

Shayla sat on the edge of the bed. "You're sure you're okay?"

"My shoulder is sore, but mostly my dignity is damaged. That's what I get for doing some stupid karaoke song. I knew better. I shouldn't have done it." Regret coursed through her.

"Well, the guys are waiting for us up on the Lido Deck."

Meg stared at Shayla. "You're kidding, right?"

"No. I told them I'd come down and get you. Drew was worried—"

"I'm not going up there. No way." She couldn't face anyone after that spectacle, most of all, Drew.

Shayla crinkled her nose. "Why not?"

"Because I just humiliated myself." Did Shayla not get that?

"It's not that bad." Shayla waved her hand. "Really."

Meg sat up. "Not that bad? I totally fell off that stage. In front of everyone. Including Drew."

Shayla reached out and touched Meg on the arm. "He doesn't care."

"I do." Meg wiped at her hair, still damp from the drink she spilled. "I'm going to take a shower."

Shayla made a pouty face. "But my birthday wish."

"I need to recover from what happened. Physically and mentally." Meg stood, her shoulder more painful now. "And I need to get some work done anyway. I should've stayed here in the first place and done that, like I planned." She could have avoided the whole mortifying incident if only she'd stayed in her room.

"Please come with me," Shayla begged.

Meg shook her head.

Shayla stood and set her hands on her hips. "You are *so* stubborn sometimes." She turned and trudged out the door.

A part of Meg felt bad for staying in the room, but a bigger part of her felt such disgrace that she couldn't face anyone right now. She let out a long breath, then headed to the bathroom for a hot shower.

CHAPTER FOUR

When Meg awoke the next morning, her shoulder was still sore. Her right ankle and both wrists hurt a little as well. *When I bang myself up, I do a fantastic job.*

She looked around the dark room. *I wonder what time it is.* Was she alone in her room? Had Shayla left without her? That wouldn't be such a bad thing. It would allow Meg to get a lot of uninterrupted time in on her website. She'd been so tired last night, she'd only worked on it for about thirty minutes before she fell asleep. "Shayla?"

Shayla opened the bathroom door and peeked out. "Hurry and get ready."

Meg sat up carefully in bed. "For what?"

Shayla stepped out into the room and flicked on the light. She was dressed in white shorts and a pink lace top. "We're meeting the guys and going with them to see Key West."

"What?" Meg rubbed her tender shoulder.

"Yeah. They want us to go with them and see the sights. Hemingway's house, the White House, the beach, shops. It'll be awesome."

"Uhhh, I'm not sure—"

"Don't use that excuse about last night." Shayla pointed at her. "And no working today."

"Hey, it was super embarrassing. And I could use the time to work out some kinks on my landing page. I think I'll stay here." That seemed to make the most sense.

"Oh, no. Uh, uh. You are not staying on this ship today. You are going with us into Key West," Shayla said with authority.

"But—"

"Nope." Shayla held her hand up. "I know you came at gun point. I know you don't want to be here and only came to be with me. But I'm going to make you enjoy it and be glad you came."

Shayla was nothing if not bossy—a quality Meg had learned to love over the years. "I do need to work on my website and getting everything ready for my big launch. If it isn't all ready by the end of next week, then my launch in three weeks will be a disaster."

"Okay, I'll make you a deal. You enjoy this cruise—with me—and I'll promise to be your slave and help you get ready for your launch when we get back. I'll do whatever you need me to." Shayla over-smiled.

Having some help after the cruise might make this deal worth it. And she had to admit, even though her dignity was bruised after the performance fiasco, she wanted to see Drew again. "Really?"

"Absolutely. Pinky promise." Shayla held out her finger.

"But you'll let me work on it a little on the cruise? Because I have so much to do and I'm getting stressed about it." A thread of anxiety rushed through her.

"Fine. But not today." Shayla motioned for Meg to get up. "Today, we go to Key West."

Meg reluctantly stood. "I must've been asleep when you got back last night."

"Totally snoring when I came in the door." Shayla did an unflattering reenactment.

"I don't snore that loud."

Shayla started laughing, then sobered. “But I am sorry you fell and hurt yourself. I hope you feel better.”

“I’m sure I will. At least physically.” Meg ran her fingers through her tangled hair. “Did Drew say anything about it?”

“He was very disappointed you didn’t join us last night. He was quite concerned and wanted to come check on you, but I told him to let you rest.”

Maybe Meg was overreacting to what happened. “He seems like a pretty nice guy.”

“A really nice guy,” Shayla said as she nodded.

Meg opened her closet and found a pair of black shorts and a coral tank top. Going to Key West might be just what she needed. She turned and looked at her friend. “And what about his brother?”

“Well . . . he’s super nice. Easy to talk to. A gentleman. And he’s hot.” Shayla giggled and fanned herself.

Meg grabbed brush and dragged it through her hair. “Are you falling for him?”

Shayla shrugged. “Maybe.”

“You fall in love so fast.” Meg shook her head. “And often.”

Shayla lifted an eyebrow. “And you never fall in love.”

“Not true. I was in love with Jensen.” The memory of him still popped up now and again.

“That was how many years ago?” Shayla acted like she was counting her fingers. “And he’s married now.”

“Thanks for reminding me.” Meg picked up her swimsuit. “We’re going to the beach?”

Shayla nodded, then said, “And all you’ve done lately, is go on one date with a guy and that’s it.”

“I know what I want. Why waste time going out with guys that aren’t what I want?” Meg went into the bathroom and changed into her swimsuit, then put her shorts and tank top on over her suit.

When Meg walked out into the room, Shayla said, “Dang, you look so good.”

“Thanks.” Meg was apprehensive about facing Drew. What if he said something about her fall? *If he's a gentleman, he won't say anything to embarrass me.*

Shayla checked her phone. "Uh, oh. We need to be on the Promenade Deck right now."

They rushed out of the room and took the elevator.

CHAPTER FIVE

Drew stood on the Promenade Deck, his hands in his pockets. He hadn't seen Meg since she hurried away after she fell off the stage. Part of him had wanted to chase after her to make sure she wasn't seriously injured, but Shayla had convinced him to let her go instead. Shayla insisted she'd bring Meg back and they could forget about karaoke and go to the casino or look at the shops. He'd been disappointed when Shayla returned alone.

Actually, he was more than disappointed. He spent the rest of the night in his cabin thinking about Meg. He shook his head. How did a woman he'd barely met affect him like that? He hadn't thought so much about a woman since . . . he couldn't recall. But it had been a long time. He hoped Meg was coming today. Key West wouldn't be as enjoyable without her. In fact, he wasn't sure he'd want to leave the ship unless she was coming too.

"Hi there," a feminine voice said behind him. He turned to see a woman with long red hair.

"Hello," he said politely.

"I think you owe me a drink," she said, then ran her fingers through her hair.

"I do?" He didn't remember ever meeting this woman. How could he owe her a drink? "Why is that?"

She leaned in toward him. "Because when I saw you, I dropped mine." She fluttered her eye lids.

A pick-up line? Really? Is this what men do to women? He laughed because he wasn't sure what else to do.

"There are some great places to visit today," Joey said as he walked up to them with a brochure in his hand.

"Hi," the woman said to Joey.

Joey dipped his head.

"So, how about that drink?" she said to Drew.

Joey gave Drew a shrewd look.

"It's early in the morning," Drew said with a smile.

"We could meet later tonight," she said as she ran her finger along his shoulder.

Drew shifted his weight. He wasn't interested in this woman at all. And he didn't want Meg to see him talking to her and get the wrong idea. It wasn't that he was ready to run off with Meg or anything like that, but he was interested in getting to know her better and spending time with her. He wasn't even sure Meg would show up, but he didn't want to risk anything by talking to this woman.

"What do you say?" she said expectantly.

Drew smiled again and said, "Thanks for the offer, but I don't think so."

WHEN THE ELEVATOR DOORS OPENED, Meg spotted Drew right away. He was wearing khaki shorts and a blue t-shirt that hugged his biceps and showed his trim mid-section. A woman with long red hair stood next to him. He smiled as he spoke to her. *I want to turn around and go back to my room.*

"He's being polite to her. That's all," Shayla whispered as they walked out of the elevator.

"Huh?" Meg tried to act as though she had no idea what Shayla was referring to.

"I know you're watching Drew and that woman."

"Oh, is Drew over there?" Meg pretended to search the crowd.

"Please." Shayla rolled her eyes, then waved at Joey.

As soon as Drew saw Meg, he moved toward her. "Hey. Good to see you."

"Hi," Meg said, worried he'd mention something about last night, but hoping he wouldn't.

"Glad you're going to join us." His face lit up.

A wave of nerves rushed through Meg.

"We're both super excited to see Key West," Shayla said.

"We can go to the Hemingway House first," Joey said.

"Oh, yeah. I love his books, especially *A Farewell to Arms*. But I also loved *The Sun Also Rises*. Oh, and his masterpiece, *For Whom the Bell Tolls*, although the violence in it is a little hard for me to read."

"My favorite Hemingway book is *The Old Man and the Sea*." Joey smiled.

Joey and Shayla continued to talk about Hemingway.

"What about you? Are you a big Hemingway fan?" Drew asked.

Meg relaxed a bit since Drew didn't say anything about last night. "No. Hemingway is too heavy for me." She preferred the happily-ever-afters.

"I'm not much for reading. I'd rather experience life than read about it." He gazed at her with his magnetic eyes, and she swallowed the nervous energy that rose from her stomach.

At this moment, real life is way better than any romance novel. And you are way more handsome than any hero in my books.

They walked out of the ship and down the narrow street. They stopped at a large building with a statue of a sailor kissing a woman in a nurse's uniform.

"Wow, that's a *huge* statue," Joey said as he looked up, shading his eyes from the morning sun.

"I think it's romantic," Shayla said.

Meg had to agree. She gazed at the tender moment caught in the sculpture.

"Looks like it's a representation of that photo taken in Times Square when the Japanese surrendered after World War II," Drew said.

Meg gazed at him.

"We did a project on World War II in high school." He shrugged.

Meg took a photo of the statue. Deep down she hoped someday she'd be swept up in a romantic moment like that. Maybe even with . . . She didn't want to finish her thought.

"I think we need to take this road to the Hemingway House," Shayla said as she pointed.

They walked along the sidewalk. The warm air was thick and full of moisture as they moved with the throng of people.

They stopped in front of a large white house with palm trees and other vegetation surrounding it. "This is the Harry S. Truman Little White House," Shayla said.

Drew tapped on his phone. "Apparently, President Truman was one of several presidents who stayed here. Truman came to recuperate after being in office about nineteen months."

"I bet that house is filled with history. What stories the walls could tell." Meg laughed.

"No kidding," Drew said.

They stood and looked at the house for several minutes.

Shayla and Joey began walking. "We want to go to the Hemingway house next."

They walked a bit farther. A long line formed outside the house.

"Do you want to go inside and see it?" Drew asked.

Meg shrugged. She wasn't a Hemingway fan and the line was long.

"Why don't we let those two go to the house and we'll keep exploring?" Drew motioned with his hand.

That was a much better option than standing in line to see that house. "Sounds good."

They separated from Shayla and Joey and walked further down the road. "How about we get something to drink?" Drew offered.

"Sure." Meg was certain a cold bottle of water would quench her thirst.

They stopped at a shop. When they got to the front, Drew asked for coconut milk. The young man at the counter handed each of them a whole coconut with a hole drilled in it and a straw sticking out.

Meg was intrigued by Drew's choice. She held the coconut and said, "Let's go outside and sit down. We can enjoy the scenery."

"I'm enjoying the scenery in here." Drew grinned, exposing his brilliant white teeth.

He's flirting with me. Meg's heartbeat sped up.

Drew led the way outside where they found a couple of chairs on the porch and sat.

"When you said we'd get a drink, I envisioned something else." Meg laughed. She'd never drunk from a whole coconut before. "This is as authentic as you get." She took a swig of the sweet milk. "Tastes coconutty."

They both laughed.

"Nothing like enjoying the island feeling." Drew sat back and crossed his ankles.

"It's nice to take some time to relax." Meg hadn't felt so at ease in a long time. Warm sunshine, music playing in the distance, and the sound of laughter floating in the air all added to the tropical feel. She could stay here all day. And with Drew at her side, maybe even longer.

"Are you a work-a-holic?" he asked, breaking into her thoughts.

Meg had to think about his question. It was true she spent more time working than anything else. It was also true that she'd put her social life on hold and focused most of her energy lately on her new business. *Work-a-holic* seemed to have a negative connotation, though. "I wouldn't say that. I'm just *motivated*." Motivated was a better word.

"Have you always been into fitness?"

She couldn't resist the opportunity to pose this question. "Do you think I have been?" She was pretty sure he'd think she had since most people assumed, based on how she looked now, that she'd been thin and fit her whole life.

He nodded. "Yeah. I'd guess you were into sports. Maybe running." That was a typical answer.

"Why do you think that?"

He seemed a little hesitant. "You look very fit."

She leaned in. "Would it surprise you to know that I was overweight all growing up? So overweight, in fact, that kids used to make fun of me and call me names."

He pulled his brows together. "Are you serious?"

"Yeah. I can still hear the teasing to this day." She tamped those memories back down, putting them in the place where she kept them most of the time. "It made me get myself into shape and eat better and motivated me to get into nutrition and fitness. I've worked hard to get into shape and be healthy."

Drew gave her a smile. "It shows."

Though the outside temperature was rising, the warmth she felt didn't come from the sun. "Thanks. Now I want to help others on their journey to better health." Enthusiasm welled up inside.

Drew peered at her.

She suddenly felt shy. "What?"

"I'm impressed, that's all."

She bit her lip, then said. "Thanks."

Drew inclined his head toward the sidewalk. "Should we make our way to the beach?"

"Sure."

Drew didn't say anything for a few minutes as they walked along underneath a canopy of leaves and vegetation. When they neared the beach, he finally said, "I really think that's amazing. To have such a strong drive to accomplish a dream is admirable."

"Thank you." She liked how Drew made her feel empowered because she was pursuing her dream.

"And to be so passionate about it."

She didn't want all the focus on her, so she said, "Sounds like you're passionate about being a chef."

He waved his hand. "I need to concentrate on my law career."

"Even if you aren't passionate about it?" She wanted him to inspire him to follow his dream.

He nodded. "My parents still have high expectations and are pretty hard on me and Joe-Joe."

"Joe-Joe?" Meg tried to stifle a laugh.

Drew did a face palm. "He's gonna hate that I let that slip out."

"It'll be our secret," Meg said with a mischievous smile.

They arrived at the small beach. The aqua water stretched out ahead of them to the horizon. A crowd spread out on the white sand and many were in the water, including lots of kids.

"Looks like everyone had the same idea," Meg said, a little disappointed she and Drew would have to share the beach with so many other people.

Drew removed his shirt and Meg's heartbeat increased at the sight of his sculpted abs and toned chest. She mentally swooned.

"Let's go for a swim," he said.

Meg took off her shorts and tank top and they made their way to the ocean. Warm water lapped at their feet as they stood on the soft, wet sand. Children splashed around them and a few couples swam out past the small waves.

The summer sun washed over them while birds flew above and laughter sounded around them. They waded out deeper and deeper. Without warning, a teenage boy ran right into Meg and nearly knocked her over. Drew caught her right before she hit the water.

"Sorry about that. I was trying to catch this Frisbee. Are you okay?" The young man with curly brown hair asked.

"I'm fine," Meg said, still in Drew's arms.

"Are you sure you're okay?' Drew asked.

Being that close to him made Meg's skin prickle and her mouth went dry. "Uh, yeah."

They stood there in each other's arms for a moment until Meg backed away. "Thanks for catching me."

"Any time." The way he said it made Meg's heart thud. She quickly reminded herself that it would be foolish to get involved with him. Sure, he was handsome, easy to talk to, and his arms were strong and sturdy as they held her, but this was a singles cruise. And singles cruises were notorious for flings that lasted only as long as the cruise. She needed to remember that. Even if she didn't want to.

"Let's swim out to that buoy," Meg said, trying to distract herself from her silly thoughts about Drew.

"You're on." Drew took several steps, then started swimming.

They reached the buoy about the same time and both of them started to tread water.

"It's great out here," Drew said.

"It is. The water is a perfect temperature." She could get use to swimming in the ocean on a regular basis.

"Glad you came after all?"

Meg gave him a look of surprise.

"Shayla said you'd need convincing."

Of course she did. Meg glanced up at the cloudless sky. "Because I was such a klutz and fell off the stage. There I said it." At least it was out in the open now.

"I wasn't going to say anything."

"I appreciate that." She started to swim back to shore because she didn't want to talk about it.

Drew swam up next to her. "It could've happened to anyone."

"But it happened to *me*." She didn't want to go back over it, so she kept swimming.

"I felt bad. I was worried you'd hurt yourself," he said over the splashing of the water as they swam.

"Can we forget it ever happened?" She wished she could go back in time and skip the whole embarrassing thing.

"It's forgotten."

As they continued swimming toward shore, Meg spotted Shayla and Joey on the beach and she reached up and waved.

It didn't take long for Shayla and Joey to meet up with them in the water. As Meg was talking to Shayla, all of a sudden Shayla's eyes grew three times their normal size. "What?" Meg said.

Shayla kept staring over Meg's shoulder.

Meg turned and saw a man, probably in his early eighties, with tanned skin wading in the water. He was wearing the tiniest Speedo she'd ever seen. But that wasn't what caught her eye. It was the set of pink fairy wings and what looked like blue evening gloves. She wanted to avert her eyes, but she couldn't.

"Have you ever seen anything like this?" Shayla asked.

"Dude, that old man," Joey said, pointing to the gentleman.

"Shhh," Shayla said.

"What? You don't think he noticed when he put on those wings and gloves?" Joey laughed.

"Don't make a scene." Shayla put her fingers up to Joey's lips.

"The things you see in Florida," Drew said.

"I think we should give him credit for feeling so comfortable in his skin," Meg said.

"Because there's so much of his skin to see. He should cover some of that up," Joey said. "I don't think that thing even qualifies as a swimsuit. It's more like a sock."

"But if he feels comfortable in it, why should we be rude about it?" Meg said. She disliked how people made others feel bad about their bodies. She'd experienced enough of that to last her the rest of her life.

“We shouldn’t,” Drew said with conviction.

"I know, let’s go explore more of the island,” Shayla said. She gave them all a cheesy smile and motioned with her head.

Meg nodded. Anything related to body shaming was definitely her hot button, but this wasn’t the time or place to get into that.

They made their way to the beach, dried off, and put their clothes back on while the summer sun bathed them in heat.

"Should we get something to eat and get into some air conditioning?" Drew said.

"We could go back to the ship and eat, then go swimming," Shayla said.

"That sounds good to me." Meg hoped they'd go back and then she could get a little time in on her website, even if her desire to work was waning.

As they walked back to the ship they made small talk about the shops and what it might be like to live on an island like this.

"Before we get back on, I'd like to go to a gift shop," Drew said.

"Me too," Shayla added. She tugged Joey with her and they disappeared into a t-shirt store.

Meg looked at Drew.

"Let’s go into that one." Drew pointed to a small storefront.

Inside there were island-themed gifts, t-shirts, jewelry, and some refrigerator magnets. Meg handled a silver bracelet with a dangly charm. She considered buying it as a memento of the day, but decided against it. She continued to look at several other items in the store, including some water bottles with a Key West insignia printed on them and a baseball cap with a sparkly palm tree.

After a few minutes, Drew walked up to the cashier. Meg couldn't see what he purchased but figured it wasn't any of her business. She continued to look around without purchasing anything.

Since Shayla and Joey were nowhere in sight, Drew said, "Let’s go back to the ship."

As they walked back toward the ocean liner, Drew cleared his throat and said, “You seemed pretty bothered by Joey’s remarks.”

Meg didn't say anything for almost a minute. "Yeah. I wish people weren't so into body shaming others. We should be focused on health."

"I agree with you."

"Like I said before, I was the target of a lot of teasing about my weight, so I was never comfortable in my own skin. Then I lost weight, but it was for the wrong reasons. It was pure vanity. After I started studying nutrition and understanding health, I realized that being thin isn't the goal, being healthy is. Exercising and eating a balanced diet are what's important, not necessarily the number on the scale." She liked sharing her feelings about weight and health with Drew.

"And you feel much better about yourself now?" Drew studied her.

"Usually. I mean, sometimes those feelings I had as a kid resurface, like when someone is being ridiculed about their body, but most of the time, I feel like I'm doing my best to take care of myself. And that's what I want to bring to others—feeling good about taking care of their bodies." She could go on and on about this subject for hours.

"You've got me sold." Drew smiled.

Meg wasn't sure if he was serious or simply placating her. "Really?" She eyed him.

"Yeah. I think taking care of ourselves is important. And your passion for it is contagious," he said with conviction.

"It is?" Warmth surrounded her heart.

"Absolutely. I predict your business will be a hit." He said it with so much enthusiasm, Meg had no problem believing him.

Once they were onboard, Meg said, "I guess I'll see you later."

"I'm counting on it." Drew's gaze caught hers.

Meg swallowed hard.

"Can we meet in an hour?" he asked, his brown eyes pulling her in.

Meg considered his request. She wanted to spend more time with him, but hesitated. After all, what was the point? Leaving this cruise with a broken heart didn't sound very appealing.

"We can eat, then go to the 80s party next to the pool." Drew tried to moonwalk, but failed miserably.

Meg bit her lip to keep from laughing. It sounded tempting—maybe too tempting. "I really need to get some work done on my website." She didn't add that her feelings for him were growing in ways she hadn't anticipated, and she wasn't sure how to deal with them.

"How about this?" His eyes lit up. "You come party with me and then I'll help you with your website."

"I'm not sure there's much you can do."

"I can give you some feedback. And you can bounce ideas off me." Drew reached out and grabbed her hand, sending a surge of tingles up her arm. "How can you resist an 80s party?" he said. "I'll even do my best Michael Jackson impression." He let go of her hand, kicked out his foot, then whirled around. He struck a typical MJ pose.

Meg laughed. "How could I possibly say no?"

"I promise you'll have time to work. In fact, I'll help you get it all ready to launch so when you leave this cruise you're ready." He took her hand again and squeezed it. "Deal?"

A smile enveloped her face. "Deal."

Meg rifled through her clothes looking for something perfect to wear. Despite her reservations, she was excited to spend more time with Drew.

"Hey, we looked for you guys," Shayla said as she flung the door open.

"Sorry. We didn't see you so we came back to the ship."

Shayla fell across her bed dramatically. "Joey is so awesome. I think I'm in love." She let out a long mournful breath.

"You fall in love all the time." Meg had lost count of how many times Shayla had made this same confession.

Shayla sat up on her elbow. "I just love *love*. There's nothing wrong with that."

"How will you know when it's the real thing?" Meg looked directly at Shayla. "You know, the 'last a lifetime' kind of thing."

"Maybe I've found it with Joey."

"Really?" Meg didn't want to be cynical, but Shayla had made such a habit out of falling in love how would she know when true love hit her?

"It could be. Besides, I'd rather fall in love too much than hardly ever." Shayla sat up and stared at Meg.

"Meaning me?"

Shayla tilted her head and shrugged.

Meg let out a laugh. "I guess we're quite a pair." She sat next to Shayla on the bed. "We'll probably both end up unmarried and sharing an apartment with a bunch of cats forever." Meg winced at the idea of being an old cat lady.

Shayla poked her in the arm. "Or we could both find love on this cruise."

"You are such a hopeless romantic." Meg shook her head. "Totally hopeless."

Shayla pointed at the lump of clothing on the floor by Meg's closet. "What are you doing?"

"I'm trying to find something to wear." She stood and walked over to the pile.

"Because?" Shayla said it with an expectant tone.

"I don't want to go to dinner naked," she said, being purposely evasive.

Shayla let out a frustrated sigh. "Come on."

"What?" Meg said coyly.

"Admit it." Shayla pointed at her.

"Fine. Drew invited me to dinner and some 80s party tonight." She gave Shayla a pained look. "Satisfied?"

“Ohhh," Shayla sang out.

Meg rolled her eyes, then asked, "What are you doing tonight?"

“Joey wants to check out the show in the theater.”

“Sounds fun.” Meg picked through her clothes, then paused and stared up at the ceiling. “What am I doing?”

“Meg?” Shayla studied her.

Meg turned and leaned back against the closet door. "I'm not sure this is a great idea.”

Shayla stood and stepped over to Meg. “To go with Drew?”

Meg nodded.

“Why not?” Shayla held out her hands.

“First of all, I have so much work to do on my website. And, secondly, I don’t need any complications right now.”

“Drew’s a *complication*?” A smile engulfed Shayla’s face. She clasped her hands together. “Finally!”

“Finally?” Meg repeated.

"You're interested—really interested—in Drew." Shayla did a few dance moves.

"I never said that.” Meg wanted to deny it.

Shayla pushed Meg’s shoulder. “Your whole body said it.”

Meg held her hand up. “Okay, okay, okay. You’re right.” She sat on the floor and crisscrossed her legs. “But I’m worried.”

“About what?” Shayla sat on the floor next to Meg.

“What if he doesn’t feel the same way?” Doubt swelled inside her like a balloon.

Shayla jerked her head back. “Are you kidding me? He’s totally into you.”

“You think so?” She hoped Shayla was right.

“Yes!” Shayla emphasized her one-word answer.

“We had a great time today.” The memory of their day together sent a ripple of warmth through her. “He’s so easy to talk to and I feel a connection to him.” A smile played at the edges of her mouth.

“This. Is. Awesome.” Shayla’s enthusiasm filled the room.

“But I don’t want to get hurt.” It’d been years since Meg had put her heart out there, but she remembered vividly the anguish she felt when Jensen left her. She wasn't anxious to repeat that.

"But if you don't take a risk, you might miss out on something spectacular," Shayla said.

"I don't know." Her heart wanted to take the chance, but her head kept getting in the way with thoughts like, *After this is over, you'll never see him again*, or *You can't fall for a guy after a few days*, or *This isn't real life, everything will be different back in the real world after the cruise.*

"You should go for it. Let yourself feel whatever you do for him. You'll never know what could happen unless you try. Right?"

Shayla had a point, but worries still floated through Meg's mind. "What happens after the cruise?"

"Don't think about that right now. Enjoy the moment. You know, smell the flowers and all that," Shayla said with fervor.

Meg chewed on her thumbnail. Perhaps Shayla was right. "It seems silly, though, that I only met him and I'm already . . ."

"What?" Shayla's eyes were as wide as the Gulf of Mexico.

"Nothing." She didn't want to admit out loud that she was falling for him—really falling—because that's exactly what was happening.

Shayla nodded with a knowing grin. "You should wear your black lace shorts."

"That's not very 80s."

"But they'll make you irresistible." Shayla raised her eyebrows.

Irresistible. That's what she wanted to be. Throwing caution to the wind, she grabbed her lace shorts and a turquoise shirt. "Here's to irresistible."

CHAPTER SIX

As Meg approached him in black shorts that showcased her shapely legs, Drew said, "You look . . . great."

No doubt, she was a beautiful woman, but that wasn't all that attracted him to her. Or made him think about her when they weren't together. There was more to her than her beauty, but he couldn't deny the strong physical attraction between them.

"Thanks." Meg tugged at her side ponytail. "This is as eighties as I get."

"I like it." Actually, he liked *her*. A lot.

"I was hoping you'd be wearing some neon-colored shirt and a mullet." She laughed.

He hadn't expected to find a woman like Meg on this cruise. He'd been focused on Joey finding someone, but Meg reminded him that he still wanted a relationship with the right woman. And maybe now was the right time.

They walked over to The Red Iguana Cantina and stood in line to order dinner. They chatted about the weather while they waited for their orders. When their food was ready, they found a small table and sat.

“I could live on Mexican food,” Meg said. “And the spicier, the better.”

Drew studied her. She kept surprising him. In good ways. “Women don’t generally enjoy spicy food.”

“I love it.”

Drew took a bite of his enchiladas. After he swallowed he said, “These are good. How about your burritos?”

“Excellent. The food on this ship is delicious.”

“Where are Joey and Shayla?” he asked more as a courtesy, because he wasn’t eager to share Meg with anyone else.

"She said they were going to catch the show in the theater, then they’d come to the party."

"They seem to be getting along well.” He took another bite.

Meg nodded, her silky ponytail falling across her shoulders.

Drew couldn’t help but wonder what it would be like to run his fingers through her long hair. He let himself hold that thought for a moment before shaking it loose. He cleared his throat and said, “Joey hasn’t been this interested in a woman since his almost-fiancée walked out on him.”

"He hasn’t dated anyone?” Meg looked at him, her brilliant blue eyes framed by dark lashes. Drew was having a hard time focusing on her words.

“I’m sorry, what was that?” he said as casually as possible.

Meg gave him a slight smile, as if she knew what he was thinking. “I asked if Joey has dated anyone.”

Drew shook his head. "Uh, no. He’s just moped around. Until now. He seems to really like Shayla."

"He should. She’s awesome.” Meg smiled, drawing Drew’s gaze to her full lips. *Stop being so distracted!*

Drew took in a quick breath. “You’ve been friends for a long time?” He sincerely wanted to know more about Shayla because Joey seemed to like her. And he wanted to learn more about Meg. He silently pledged to pay more attention to the conversation than

Meg's obvious beauty that had some kind of crazy strong pull—like a magnet. He'd never met a woman like her.

"We met in high school. She moved into my neighborhood in Dallas right before our freshman year." Meg sipped her water.

Childhood memories swirled around Drew's mind. "I used to live in Dallas when I was a kid. Then my dad moved us to Austin."

Meg wiped at her mouth. "Why did you move to Austin?"

Drew tore his gaze from her lips and said, "My dad. He opened a law practice in Austin."

"You graduated from high school in Austin?"

"Yeah, then went to A&M for my undergraduate and for law school. I was offered a job in Dallas, and since Joey had already moved back, I did too." He took another bite.

"How does your dad feel about that?" Meg asked, her gaze intent on him.

"He keeps trying to get both of us to come back to Austin, but I think we all have a much better relationship now." Drew wanted a better relationship with his dad, but he didn't want the constant nit-picking and intense pressure that came when he lived in Austin. He'd never discussed his relationship with his dad with anyone before, but he liked being able to talk to Meg about it.

"If you stay in Dallas, you can open a restaurant there, right?" Meg smiled and Drew's stomach instantly reacted. This woman was really getting to him.

"I don't know about that," he said. Opening a restaurant would be a giant risk.

"Well, I think you should." Meg leaned in and a whiff of her warm, spicy perfume tickled his nose. "And I'll be the first in line to try it."

He leaned in closer to her, his pulse racing. "I'd like that." He'd been hesitant to share his dream with anyone, but, somehow, Meg made him feel not only comfortable enough to share his dream with her, but the way she reacted made him feel like it wasn't so impossible after all. Meg made him feel like he could do anything.

"I'd like that too," she said softly.

For a moment, their gazes connected and all he could think about was tugging her close, cupping her chin in his hand, then laying his lips across hers and kissing her until they docked again in Galveston.

"There you guys are," Shayla said, interrupting the moment.

Meg sat back, exhaling an almost imperceptible breath, but Drew saw it. "I thought you were going to the show," she said.

Shayla looked between the two of them. "Did I interrupt something?"

Drew wanted to shout that, yes, she'd interrupted something and could she please go away. Instead he kept his gaze on Meg.

Meg cleared her throat, then waved her hand. "No. Nothing." She flicked a quick glance at Drew.

"Well, we decided we were hungry and an 80s party sounded better than the Musical Revue," Shayla said. She and Joey sat at the table.

WHILE THEY ATE DINNER, everyone chatted, but Meg kept thinking back to her conversation with Drew right before Shayla and Joey arrived. Had she sounded too forward? Or like she expected to see him after the cruise? Because she didn't want him to think that. Unless he thought the same thing. But if he didn't, she didn't want to sound presumptuous. Because they might not ever see each other again. Except, she wanted to see him. Did he want to see her? *Wow. I'm a hot mess.*

There was a moment when it almost seemed like Drew was going to kiss her. How did she feel about that? As she snuck a glance at him across the table while he spoke to his brother, she was pretty sure she'd kiss him back. Meeting someone she was interested in, was the last thing she expected to happen on this cruise.

"What do you think, Meg?" Shayla said, tapping Meg on the arm.

"Uh, what?"

"I asked if you wanted me to get you a drink." Shayla gave her big eyes.

"No, thanks. I'm fine." Meg snuck another glance at Drew. He was animated as he talked with Joey, then the two of them laughed. She admired the closeness they seemed to share as brothers.

After they finished eating, Joey suggested they take a stroll around the Lido Deck. It was a perfect night for a walk under the twinkling stars, especially with Drew.

"Let's go toward the front of the ship," Drew said. He extended his hand for Meg and she slipped hers inside. When his fingers gently closed around hers, a ripple of electricity traveled up her arm.

"What's the front of the ship called again?" Shayla asked.

"The aft?" Joey said.

"Nah. I think it's the bow," Drew said.

"What's the starboard side?" Shayla asked. "That sounds kind of romantic."

Joey pointed to their left.

Meg looked at Drew. "Is he right?"

Drew shrugged. "I only know the front and back." He laughed and it made Meg want to laugh as well.

When they reached an area near the front, they stopped next to the railing. The moon's reflection bounced across the water and the salty, sea breeze blew through Meg's hair.

"This is great, isn't it?" Shayla asked. "Aren't you glad you came?" She elbowed Meg.

Meg turned to her and said, "Yes. You win. I'm glad I came."

"I'm glad you came too," Drew said.

A shiver ran down Meg's back and it wasn't from the gentle wind.

"What about tomorrow?" Joey asked. "We're going to Freeport. Something like that." He slung his arm around Shayla's shoulders. "We should go to the beach."

"Ooo. Yeah, let's go snorkeling." Shayla smiled.

"We could book one of the shore excursions. I saw one with snorkeling," Drew said. "You in?" He gazed at Meg.

Going to a beach with a handsome man that made her heart flutter sounded fantastic, but she didn't want to sound too eager. "A beach? In the Bahamas? Hmm. I'm not sure."

Drew studied her.

Meg playfully tapped him on the arm. "Kidding, of course. I'd love to go with you." She knew she should be spending time working on her website, but being with Drew made that fall right out of her head.

Drew pointed to a constellation above them. "Orion."

Meg searched the sky and squinted at the stars above them. "I can't see it."

Drew moved behind Meg, his warm breath on her neck making her skin prickle. He gently lifted her hand and pointed it toward the night sky. "See those three stars in a row?"

Meg narrowed her eyes. "Those right there?"

"Yes. That's his belt." He took her hand and drew an outline of Orion.

"I'm not very good at finding any of these. I can never find the Big or Little Dipper," she said apologetically.

Meg leaned her head back against Drew's solid shoulder. Drew wrapped his arms around her as she gazed up at the black velvet sky. They stood there in silence, immersed in the moment. Everything, and everyone, around them seemed to disappear and she didn't want to move any time soon. Actually, she didn't want to move from that spot. Ever.

Is it possible I've met someone I could possibly see a future with? On a singles cruise. Never thought that would happen.

Over the sound system a deep voice interrupted Meg's reverie. "It's me, Matteo. Are you guys ready for a gnarly good time? We're starting our 80s Funtastic Party right now, next to the pool on the Lido Deck. Come join us for some radical and tubular fun."

Shayla sidled up to Meg and said, "Let's go to the party!" She raised her hands above her head and shook them while Joey watched her and smiled.

Hand-in-hand, Meg and Drew walked back toward the music.

"Come on, everyone." Matteo gestured with his hands for people to gather in. "This will be totally, like, so awesome tonight. So rad."

"He's really got that Valley Girl vibe going," Drew said with a laugh.

Meg nodded. The only vibe she had going was wanting to be with Drew—talking to him, listening to him, feeling his arms around her, being so close to him she could inhale his musky cologne, and even kissing him. A little warning voice sounded in her head, but she silenced it.

The crowd started clapping.

"We're going to start our dance party with some neon jewelry." He threw out some plastic sticks into the group standing near him. Drew caught a couple of them. "Put them on your wrists and around your neck so we can get this party going," Matteo said as he swiveled his hips and raised his arms in the air.

Drew snapped each stick to ignite the glowing substance inside. He held one out and said, "A bracelet for you."

Meg extended her arm and he placed the glowing bracelet on her.

"Now your necklace." He stepped around behind her, then reached his arms in front of her with the glow stick in his hands. "I'll put it on for you." Drew connected the necklace, his fingers grazing her neck and making her skin erupt in millions of goose bumps. He let his fingers linger for a moment.

When Meg turned around, their gazes locked, sending her heart plummeting to her stomach.

"How about some Cyndi Lauper? She'll start us out with 'Girls Just Want to Have Fun.'" Matteo started to sing with the music.

Shayla came over and started dancing. "Come on. Let's dance." She shimmied next to Meg.

Meg decided to join her and the two of them danced back-to-back. Meg could feel Drew's gaze on her. When she looked up, he smiled. A steady river of heat spread through her until it reached the top of her head and slid all the way down to her toes. He moved closer to her.

"I think I'll take your dance partner and make her mine," he said to Shayla.

Make her mine. Meg liked the way those words sounded together.

They all danced to a few more songs by Wham, Madonna, and Phil Collins. Meg hadn't had this much fun in a very long time. In fact, she was trying to remember the last time she felt so carefree. When "Ghostbusters" came on they all sang to it.

"We're gonna slow down the party for a moment now with Lionel Richie and his 1984 hit song, 'Hello,'" Matteo said. "Dudes, grab that girl next to you and hold her tight."

Drew pulled Meg in close and they began to sway to the music. The words of the song floated on the air around her while his strong arms held her. *Am I who he's looking for?* She had to push that thought out and remind herself she'd only just met him, even though, somehow, she felt like she'd known him so much longer. As they moved to the sensual rhythm of a song that was older than she was, Meg's mind entertained silly thoughts. Thoughts that made her giddy and light. Thoughts she shouldn't be thinking, but couldn't stop from popping into her head.

"I like this song," Drew said. "It's an oldie but goodie."

"I like it too." She more than liked it, she was beginning to love this song.

Drew pulled back enough to peer into Meg's eyes. "I'm having a great time on this cruise."

"Me too."

"I didn't expect to. I mean, I wanted Joey to have fun, but, well, I only came along to, you know, make sure he enjoyed it. But, I . . . well . . . I'm glad I came."

Meg smiled at the way he stumbled over some of his words. It sounded as if he was trying to express his feelings for her. "I feel the same way."

Drew's gaze slipped to her mouth and suddenly her heartbeat exploded inside her chest. *Is he going to kiss me? In front of everyone?*

Someone tapped Meg on the shoulder. "Hey, we want to go get some ice cream. Do you want to come?" Shayla asked.

Meg wanted to strangle Shayla for interrupting, once again. Instead, she cleared her throat and said, "If Drew wants to." She eyed him.

"Uh, sounds good. I guess." He seemed a little dazed.

She and Drew followed Shayla and Joey into the restaurant area where a soft serve ice cream dispenser sat. They each got a cone, filled it with ice cream, then found a table next to the window.

"I was getting too hot dancing," Shayla said.

"Me too," Meg said with a smile. She glanced at Drew and he winked, making her stomach flip-flop.

"Nothing better than an ice cream cone," Shayla said as she took a big lick.

"I wish they had pistachio ice cream," Joey said.

"Pistachio? As soft serve?" Shayla wrinkled her nose.

"Yeah. Pistachio."

"Ew."

Shayla and Joey continued to talk about ice cream. Drew licked his ice cream but said nothing as he peered at Meg with his intensely magnetic eyes. She willed her heart to slow its erratic beat. All she could think about was dancing with Drew. Holding Drew. Kissing Drew. It was almost too much to sit there next to him without flinging her arms around him.

"Hey," Shayla said. She glanced between the two of them, then let out a whistle.

"What?" Meg said.

"Should we leave the two of you alone?" Shayla asked.

Meg wiped at her warmed cheek. "No. Why? We're only eating ice cream."

Shayla raised her eyebrows. "Well, Joey and I are going back to the dance party."

"We are too," Drew said without taking his eyes off Meg.

"Yeah," Meg said, her gaze glued to Drew's.

Arms around each other, Meg and Drew made their way back to the party. They danced to a few more fast songs.

"I'm getting tired," Drew said. "Are you interested in slowing things down and taking a walk around the ship?"

"Sure." A walk with Drew—in the moonlight—sounded perfect.

She slid her hand inside his, marveling at how her hand felt like it belonged there. She'd been set to work through most of this cruise, but meeting Drew had changed that.

"I'm looking forward to snorkeling tomorrow," he said.

"It sounds fun. I haven't ever snorkeled before." She didn't care what they did together, as long as they were together.

"It's pretty easy. I'll help you."

"I'd like that." Swimming in the ocean with Drew sounded like a dream.

They stopped by the railing. Drew turned to her and said, "I think I owe you an apology."

"You do?" She searched her mind for why he might need to apologize, but there was nothing.

"I think I might be keeping you from working on your website." He rested his hand on her shoulder.

She shrugged, trying to remember if she even had a website.

He let his hand slide down her arm, then took her hand in his. "I still want to look at it, if you'll let me."

Being so close to Drew twisted her thoughts into a pretzel. Finally, she said, "What about tomorrow when we get back from the shore excursion?"

"Definitely."

He took another step toward her, making her breath catch in her throat. All she could think about was being with Drew and feeling his lips on hers. He reached up and brushed an errant strand of hair from her face, then let his finger trail down her cheek to her neck. Every part of her jumped to attention.

He placed his hand at the small of her back and tugged her gently to him. She could feel the heat of his breath on her lips. She knew a kiss was imminent and her lips pleaded for it. Yearned for it. Craved it. Like nothing else.

He brushed his lips lightly across hers, making her knees feel as if they'd buckle at any moment. Again, he grazed her lips, then gently laid his mouth on hers. The kiss was almost timid at first, as if he were asking permission. When she leaned into him, the kiss became stronger, more confident. As his lips searched hers, an electrifying sensation traveled throughout her body, alerting all her senses. She'd never felt so alive before. She wanted to drink in every drop of this kiss as their lips danced a passionate tango.

Finally, Drew pulled back and let out a breath. "Wow," he said.

She grabbed the railing trying to steady herself from the dizzying effects.

"That was some kiss." He shook his head slightly.

Meg smiled. "I'm glad you liked it."

Loud laughter rang through the air and they both turned. Two couples, obviously tipsy, were walking toward them. One of the women tripped and fell to the ground. Drew rushed over to her. "Can I help you?"

One of the men pushed Drew away. "That's my woman. Hands off. Or I'll . . ." He didn't finish his sentence.

"I was only trying to help," Drew said.

The woman pushed her long black hair out of her face. She started laughing and slung her arms around Drew's neck. "I like you. You're cute."

Meg wasn't sure what to do, so she stood there stunned.

Drew untangled the woman's arms. "I think you've had too much to drink."

The portly man grabbed the woman. "Come on. Let's go."

She fell into the man's arms, then waved at Drew. "Okay. Let's get some more drinks."

The couples walked past, and Drew came back over to Meg.

"Looked like that guy was going to punch you," Meg said.

Drew shrugged. "I was only trying to help her after she fell."

"Hey, Meg," Shayla shouted from down the walkway.

Meg waved at Shayla. More than anything she wanted to have more time with Drew, but the moment was gone. Again.

"The party is over. Where have you been?" Shayla asked, raising her eyebrow up.

Meg tried to conceal her smile.

"We've been getting to know each other," Drew said.

"Oh, is that what you call it?" Shayla said, then laughed. "What time is the shore excursion tomorrow?"

"We dock at the port about eight o'clock in the morning and we're supposed to meet at eight thirty," Drew said.

"I can't wait," Shayla said with a wide grin.

Joey put his arm around her. "This cruise is the best idea I've ever had."

"You?" Drew said. He reached over and slugged Joey in the arm.

"Yeah, me. You've been no fun for so long. Glad I talked you into coming." Joey laughed, his brown eyes full of mischief.

Drew shook his head. "Something like that."

Shayla's phone chirped.

"What is that?" Meg asked.

Shayla pulled out her phone. "Oh, yeah. I made a reservation for us to get a massage." She pointed at Meg.

"Tonight? Isn't it too late?" Even though a message sounded heavenly, Meg wasn't at all eager to leave Drew.

"They were offering a special late-night deal, so I bought it. I forgot to tell you. Sorry." Shayla gave her a cheesy smile. "Please, come with me."

Meg wanted to spend more time with Drew, but she didn't want to disappoint Shayla. She glanced over at Drew and shrugged.

"You two should get your massages. We'll meet you in the morning for breakfast," Joey said.

Shayla gave Joey a hug. "See you in the morning."

Drew stepped close to Meg and whispered in her ear, "I'd rather spend more time with you."

Meg nodded.

"I'll see you in the morning." His warm breath tickled her ear and made goosebumps erupt along her neck.

Meg and Shayla made their way to an upper deck and went in to the massage area. A petite Asian woman greeted them and showed them where to put on robes to prepare for their massages.

As they were lying on the tables, Shayla said, "So?"

"So, what?"

"You and Drew." Shayla practically sang it out.

Trying to prevent a smile from exploding on her face, Meg said, "What?"

Shayla rose up on her elbow. "There is so much electricity between you two that you could power a small city."

"Really?" Just thinking about Drew made Meg's heartbeat race.

Shayla waved her other hand. "Oh yeah."

"He kissed me."

Shayla's eyes widened. "He did?"

A smile, so big it hurt her cheeks, spread across Meg's face.

"And you loved it." Shayla's face brightened.

"I did." Meg sat up. "It was fantastic. Better than fantastic. *The* best kiss I've ever had." The memory sent a chill down her spine.

"For real?" Shayla also sat up.

"Yeah. I feel like I've been run over by a truck or something. I can't even think straight." Meg had never experienced such strong feelings, especially in such a short time.

"Wow, you've totally fallen for him."

"I think I have." There it was, out in the stratosphere. Despite this being a cruise of losers and Meg's resistance to meeting anyone, somehow, she'd found the perfect man. It was nothing short of miraculous.

Two Asian women came into the room and Shayla and Meg both lay back down. The Asian women began to massage Meg and Shayla.

"What about you and Joey?" Meg asked while the woman worked the knot out of her mid-back.

"He's great and funny and fun. I like talking to him." Shayla sounded excited, but there was hint of something in her voice.

"But?"

Shayla let out a long breath. "I don't think he's over his broken heart. He wants to be, but he isn't. I don't want to push him."

Meg wasn't sure what to say. After a few moments, she simply said, "I'm sorry."

"Don't be. We might not make a love connection, but we can have a good time together on this cruise. And maybe when his heart is completely healed, we'll see each other again. I don't know. I'm just happy you've found someone."

"I don't know if we'll see each other after the cruise." Meg didn't want to get her hopes up.

"Seriously? Of course you will. Anyone can see there's something amazing between you."

Meg thought for a moment while the woman massaged her shoulders. She wanted to voice her concerns, but wasn't sure how to put them into words. Finally, she said, "It seems too good to be true. He seems too good to be true. Maybe—"

"No maybes," Shayla said, cutting her off. "Stop stressing out about it. Just see where it goes."

Meg was surprised at how much she liked Drew and how fast it had happened. Perhaps Shayla was right, and she needed to enjoy the time with him and stop worrying. "I really do like him."

Shayla giggled. "I know. And he likes you. Let yourself enjoy this."

Meg closed her eyes and pondered on Shayla's words while she savored the rest of her massage.

After they finished their massages, as Meg and Shayla walked back to their room, Meg felt relaxed and at ease. The massage was fantastic and she was looking forward to the day tomorrow. When they arrived at their stateroom, Meg found a piece of paper taped to the door with her name on it.

"A love note?" Shayla sang out.

Meg's fingers fumbled at the paper as she unfolded it. Inside, it read, "I'm looking forward to tomorrow. Drew." Meg clutched it to her chest.

"What did it say? What did it say?" Shayla bounced up and down.

Meg smiled while anticipation surged through her.

DREW STARED at the ceiling while Joey snored another chorus. He'd expected some superficial fun at best on this cruise. Instead, he'd connected with a woman he could see a future with.

Whoa.

For so long, he'd avoided a relationship and concentrated on his career—a career that paid his bills and made his father happy, but didn't bring him much satisfaction. Talking to Meg about being a chef had brought out feelings he'd tucked away for years about his career choice and his life's path.

Was it possible he could forge a new path? One that included Meg and being a chef? His mind went to work conjuring up scenarios. He had enough savings to finance opening a restaurant. But he wasn't a master chef. He loved to cook and create dishes, but he hadn't had any formal training—his father would never have approved of that. Still, as the owner of a restaurant, he would create the menu and prepare any meals he wished.

Dallas was a great spot for restaurants. He could open an Italian one and use some family recipes as well as new ones. He thought about the décor and even a name. His excitement welled up and he decided he'd write a rough business plan first thing in the morning. He couldn't wait to share this with Meg. After all, talking to her had put all these other thoughts into motion.

Coming on this cruise was the best decision he'd made in a long time. He'd reignited his passion for cooking and his dream of owning a restaurant and, even better, he'd found Meg.

CHAPTER SEVEN

Meg awoke before her alarm went off. She jumped out of bed and rushed into the small bathroom to brush her teeth. Fixing her hair into a high ponytail with some wisps around her face, she swiped on some waterproof mascara and added some highlighter to her cheeks. After she finished, she rummaged through her clothes to find her red-and-white striped swimsuit and a white lace cover-up. She put on her clothes and spritzed her neck with her favorite perfume, then walked back out into the room.

"What time is it?" Shayla said but didn't move.

"Time to get going so we can start our adventure for the day. I can't wait to see all the tropical fish while we snorkel." Of course, the best part would be spending the day with Drew.

Shayla sat up in bed, then fell back over to the side. "Can't we keep sleeping for another hour, or five?"

Meg walked over to Shayla's bed. "Come on sleepyhead, get out of bed. We're supposed to meet the guys in less than thirty minutes. I'm all ready." Energy sizzled through her.

"Do you think it's weird we've done a role reversal?" Shayla moved her tangled hair from in front of her face. "I mean, I was the one trying to get you motivated when we first came aboard and now you're like Little Mary Sunshine anxious to get to breakfast."

Meg raised her eyebrows. She knew why her attitude had changed and who was to blame. "Get up! We don't want to be late for snorkeling. It's going to be amazing." Sure, the scenery would be breathtaking, but that's not what would catch her eye.

Shayla rose from bed, stretched her arms above her head, and let out an audible yawn.

"You don't have much time," Meg said, clapping her hands.

"Don't you need to work on your website for a little while or something?"

My website. Oh yeah. She hadn't thought about her business at all recently. Only Drew had been on her mind, but Shayla was right. She needed to spend at least a little time on it, because she still had a launch date she needed to meet. "Yes, actually. I'll work on it while I wait for you."

Shayla went into the bathroom and Meg fired up her laptop. She tapped her fingers on the keyboard and found her website. She stared at the screen, but didn't really see it. Her thoughts kept circling back to Drew, and her anticipation for today's activities swelled until she thought she'd burst. *Stop it. Focus on the website.*

Again, she set her gaze on the computer screen. All the words seemed to run together and the colors swirled around. She saw Drew's face everywhere she looked. Finally, she shut the laptop off. It was no use. She couldn't possibly concentrate on anything as long as thoughts of Drew danced across her mind.

Meg sat back and stared out into space, a smile enveloping her face. *Is this what it feels like to be in love? Wait. Love? No. Not love. Like.* She was in *like*. Whatever it was, it made her feel light and giddy and happy.

"Wow, you've got it so bad," Shayla said.

Meg blinked. "How long have you been standing there?"

"Long enough."

"Isn't this what you wanted? That I'd find a guy?" Shayla had been harping on Meg to find a man for forever.

Shayla nodded. "Yeah. I'm just shocked. I've been trying to get you to date for so long I was beginning to think it'd never happen."

"I've been on dates." Meg said it with mock indignation.

Shayla held her hands up. "I'll rephrase. I've been trying to get you to have a relationship for years."

Meg smiled.

"I'm glad you've met Drew and, even more, I'm glad you're willing to give him a chance."

Meg stood and grabbed her sunglasses. "Hurry and get ready so we can go."

DREW SAT at a table waiting for Meg to show up. His heartbeat increased the moment he saw her walking toward him. *Whatever this is, I like it.*

"Where's Joey?" Shayla asked.

"He went to check on the excursion and ask a couple of questions."

"I'm excited to go snorkeling, but a little scared. I hope there aren't any sharks," Meg said as she sat next to him, the faint, spicy scent she wore inviting him to move in closer.

"No worries. I'll protect you." That sounded pretty lame. He mentally gave himself a facepalm.

She smiled at him and said, "I hope so."

"Uh, should we get breakfast or are you two interested in eating?" Shayla asked.

Meg giggled and it made Drew smile.

"I'm famished," Drew said.

Joey walked up to the table. "We're going to Pirate's Cove. We should be able to see plenty of fish. We need to meet the shuttle out by the dock."

"When?" Shayla asked.

Joey looked at his watch. "In forty-five minutes."

"Let's get eating then," Drew said, his stomach rumbling.

They piled up their plates with food from the buffet and sat at a table.

"Do you think we'll see any turtles?" Shayla asked.

"We might." Joey took a sip of his orange juice. "We may see all sorts of sea life."

"Sounds exciting," Meg said.

Drew couldn't help but smile as he watched Meg. She did something to his heart, and while seeing different sea life sounded intriguing, Drew was only interested in spending the day with Meg. He didn't care if they were snorkeling on an exotic island or sitting on a couch in sweats. As long as he could be with Meg, it didn't matter.

"What?" Meg said, breaking into his thoughts. She eyed him with a half-smile tugging at her mouth.

"Nothing." He tried to act nonchalant.

"You were watching me," she whispered.

Busted. He scratched his head, then said, "Guilty as charged."

"Why?"

He cleared his throat. "Because I meant what I said in that note."

Her cheeks colored and she bit her lip—an endearing habit he noticed she had.

Shayla and Joey continued to talk about the snorkeling trip. Drew continued to watch Meg, memorizing every feature of her face.

Shayla stood. "We should go."

Joey also stood, then whispered something to her and she laughed.

Drew didn't have to ask any questions, he already knew it was about Meg and him.

"What?" Meg said.

Shayla waved her hand. "Joey told me a funny joke."

"We want to hear it," Meg said.

"It's nothing," Joey said, exchanging a smile with Shayla.

"I think we're ready to go," Drew said as he stood. He wanted to divert Meg's attention.

Meg took another sip of her orange juice. "Let's go."

CHAPTER EIGHT

They boarded the shuttle to Pirate's Cove. Meg and Drew sat next to each other and he slipped his arm around her. She snuggled into it, enjoying the relaxing, easy feel of being with him.

When they arrived at their destination, they followed a middle-aged man with a black goatee. He led them to an area where they put on their snorkeling gear and swim shirts. The summer sun streamed down all around them and reflected on the clear blue water. They spent the next couple of hours swimming near a reef and watching all sorts of colorful fish.

After they finished, they found a spot on the white sand beach and spread out their towels.

"That was incredible," Meg said.

"So many gorgeous fish out there," Shayla said. "But no turtles." She made a pouty face.

"Maybe tomorrow we can find a place to see turtles when we go to Nassau," Joey said. "I'll do my best to find you a turtle."

"Really?"

He nodded.

"You're so sweet." Shayla threw her arms around him and kissed him on the cheek. Joey turned, then kissed Shayla on the lips.

Meg and Drew turned to each other to give Shayla and Joey some privacy, even though they didn't seem to care that they were kissing in front of everyone.

"Is that their first kiss?" Drew asked quietly.

"I think so." Meg wasn't sure, but the last time she'd talked to Shayla things between them weren't moving in that direction. Something must've changed while they were snorkeling.

"Good. I'm glad they're hitting it off." Drew wore a satisfied grin. The kind of grin that made Meg want to kiss him, but she resisted. She didn't want to push anything, not when things were so new and delicate.

"Me too," she said. "And I'm glad I wore this swim shirt. Otherwise I'd be burned to a crisp by now. And a sunburn on this cruise wouldn't be much fun."

"No, I don't think it would. It might limit our activities." Drew gave a sly smile and it sent a shiver down her spine. She wouldn't want to miss out on any opportunities to feel his arms around her.

"You know, I've been thinking," Drew said, sifting some sand through his fingers.

"About what?" She hoped he'd been thinking about the two of them.

After a few moments, he said, "Opening a restaurant."

"Really?" Her disappointment that he wasn't talking about their relationship was tempered with her enthusiasm. She wanted Drew to pursue his dream.

"This cruise has inspired me. I wrote up a crude business plan this morning," he said with an endearing bashfulness.

"I'd love to read it." Meg wanted to encourage him.

Drew glanced at her from under thick, long eyelashes. "I'd like that."

"What kind of restaurant?"

"Italian. Like a bistro." Drew inhaled slightly. "Bistro Italiano."

"I like it." She nodded. "I'd definitely eat there."

Drew gazed out at the ocean. "I have a menu in mind already."

Meg smiled at his eagerness.

"And the décor. It'll look like people are sitting in an Italian garden." He looked at Meg and his eyes lit up. "I haven't felt this way about business. Ever."

"I'm so glad." She loved seeing the excitement splayed across his handsome face.

He reached over and placed his warm hand across hers, making her quiver at his touch. "And I owe it to you."

"Me? This is your idea." She didn't want to take credit that didn't belong to her.

He peered at her and she tried not to lose herself in the depth of his eyes. "But you made me think about it again with your questions. And ever since then, I haven't been able to stop thinking of all the possibilities. I might even do some catering," he said with such fervor that it was contagious.

"When do you think you'll start?"

His expression sobered, and he sat back. "Therein lies the big problem. My dad will flip when he finds out."

"Maybe he'll be supportive?" she said with as much optimism as possible.

"Not likely." He let out a long breath. "I'll just have to figure out how to make it work."

"If you follow your dream, you won't be disappointed." She believed this and wanted him to believe it as well.

Drew leaned in close. "Thank you."

"You're welcome," she whispered, her heart beating erratically in anticipation.

He put his hand under her chin and tugged her closer to him, then gently brushed her lips with his. She moved in and reached her hand up around his neck. The heat of the sun couldn't compare to the fire in his kiss and the burning sensation it sent zipping throughout her body. She could make this a permanent habit.

"Hey, you two, we need to meet our shuttle. If you can separate your lips long enough." Shayla laughed.

Meg turned to her and said, "You should talk."

Shayla shrugged.

After they took the shuttle back to the boat, they agreed to spend some time taking showers and getting ready for the semi-formal captain's dinner.

"I THOUGHT you said Joey wasn't ready for a relationship," Meg said while she towel-dried her hair.

"I guess I was wrong. That kiss on the beach was amazing." Shayla pulled a flowered dress over the top of her head. "And you two were about to set the beach on fire."

Meg smiled. "He is the best kisser. Ever. I think I could kiss him for the rest of time. And even longer than that." The memory of his kisses made Meg's heart do cartwheels.

"You're welcome," Shayla said, wearing a smug expression.

"Yeah, yeah, yeah. I know. If it weren't for you, I would've never come on this cruise. I'll name my first child after you."

Shayla jerked her head back. "Wow, this is more serious than I thought."

"No. I didn't mean." Meg waved her hands. "Wait, what I meant was. Never mind. Forget it." It was just a figure of speech. She wasn't actually thinking about marrying Drew and having kids with him. That would be ridiculous. Beyond ridiculous. They'd barely met. Marriage? No way. At all. Right?

"You look gorgeous in that blue dress," Shayla said, breaking into Meg's internal freak out. "Makes your eyes look so dramatic."

Meg sucked in a calming breath. "Thanks. I hope Drew likes it." She smoothed the dress.

“You don’t have to hope anything. He’ll like it.” Shayla raised her eyebrows. “Actually, he’ll love it.”

Shaking her head, Meg said, “Did you think we’d find two great guys on this cruise?”

“Truthfully? No.” Shayla laughed. “But I’m glad we did.”

“Me too.”

CHAPTER NINE

While buttoning his grey dress shirt, Drew said, "Things are good with Shayla?"

"I really like her. A lot. She makes me laugh and we have a good time together. I can see us dating when we get back. What about you and Meg?" Joey put on a burgundy tie.

"I definitely see us dating." He'd never felt so sure about a woman before.

Joey grabbed his black suit coat, then gazed at Drew. "Who knew."

Drew adjusted the collar of this shirt. "What?"

"That my big brother could fall so fast."

"Hey. I didn't say I've fallen." He liked Meg. A lot. But he hadn't fallen for her. He wasn't in love. Not. Even. Close. They'd date after the cruise and see where it went. That was all. Because no one falls in love on a cruise ship. And not after a few days. That's not possible. Or logical.

"You've totally fallen for her." Joey grinned and clapped Drew on the shoulder.

Drew put on his tie and adjusted it in the mirror. Joey was wrong.

Wasn't he? Whatever Drew felt about Meg, it was good. Very good. And he liked it. He liked how she made him feel when they were together. He liked how she'd reignited his passion about owning a restaurant. He liked talking to her. Listening to her. Laughing with her. Holding her. Kissing her.

Maybe he had fallen.

All he knew, was that he couldn't wait to get to dinner so he could spend more time with Meg.

"THERE THEY ARE." Shayla waved at Joey and Drew.

Meg's heart jumped into her throat when she saw Drew in his charcoal suit, dress shirt, and teal-and-black striped tie. How could he be even more attractive?

"You look so beautiful tonight," Drew said as he sat next to Meg.

"Thank you." The tips of her ears warmed. "You look very nice as well." *Very nice? Make that very attractive—so attractive I can't think about anything else.*

He smiled. "After dinner, let's go dancing at the Moonlight Club."

"I'd love you." *Oh. No. Did I just say I'd love* you? *Seriously?* She wanted to smack herself in the mouth and then disappear into oblivion.

"What did you say?" Drew leaned in.

"I said that I'd love to. Go dancing. Tonight." She hoped he didn't hear what she actually said, but the smile on his face made her suspect otherwise.

I can't believe I said that. What an idiot.

A tall waiter with a receding hairline came to the table. He shared the specials for the captain's dinner, then took their orders for appetizers and the main course.

"I've never tried oysters before," Meg said. "I hope I like them."

"They look disgusting," Shayla said, then visibly shuddered.

"They're good. You can trust me," Drew said. He reached his arm around Meg and she relaxed into it as if it were the most natural thing in the world.

"Remember when Dad took us to that one restaurant and we tried oysters for the first time?" Joey said.

"Ah, yes. I was twelve or thirteen, maybe." Drew laughed.

Joey tapped his forehead. "What was the name of the restaurant?"

Drew sat back. "Shasta something."

"Shasta's Sea Shack?" Meg said.

"Yeah, that was it." Drew nodded, then sipped his water.

"We had one of those near my house when I was a teenager." Meg recalled going there several times.

"Really?" Drew cocked his head.

She nodded.

"Because it was near our house, too," Drew said.

"Interesting. Maybe there's more than one?" Meg said.

"We actually lived in Flower Mound, right outside Dallas," Joey said. "It's northwest of Dallas."

The waiter brought some rolls and placed them on the table. Joey grabbed one and so did Shayla.

"Wait. You lived in Flower Mound?" Meg looked at Drew. "So did I."

"Small world," Joey said as he buttered his roll.

"We lived in Flower Mound until I was in seventh grade. Then we moved to Austin." Drew took another sip of his water.

"Wow. I can't believe we lived in the same town." Meg was surprised they'd both lived in the same suburb of Dallas.

"Maybe you went to the same school. Wouldn't that be funny?" Shayla said with a smile.

Meg blinked. "Which schools did you attend?"

"Uh, let me think." He smiled. "It's been a long time."

"We went to Donald Elementary," Joey said.

"Then I went to McKamy Middle School. I haven't thought about that school for years. Feels like a lifetime ago." Drew sat back and laughed.

"I went to McKamy," Meg said. "Small world."

"Seriously? You guys went to the same school? I was only kidding." Shayla glanced between them. "This must be fate."

"I'm sure we didn't have any classes together," Drew said. "I would've remembered you."

"And I don't remember any Drews," Meg said, trying to recall if she'd ever seen him.

"He wasn't Drew back in the day," Joey said with a laugh.

The waiter approached their table, then set down their appetizers. On Meg's plate sat some shells with what looked like a pile of mucous on top. Her stomach turned while she poked one of them with her fork.

"Like I said, disgusting." Shayla crinkled her nose.

"You should try it," Drew said.

"You first." Meg pushed her plate toward him.

Drew took one of the shells and slurped up the oyster. "Delicious." He picked one up. "Your turn."

Meg drew in a breath of courage and took the shell from Drew. She brought it close to her mouth, but everything in her said to get it as far away from her as possible. There was nothing appetizing about it.

"I'll pay you twenty bucks if you eat that," Shayla said.

Meg squeezed her eyes tight and in one swift movement sucked in the oyster. As the ball of slime hit her tongue, she wanted to gag, but didn't want to embarrass herself. She swallowed it, then grabbed her ice water and chugged it down.

"I didn't think you'd do it," Shayla said.

"It was pretty good, right?" Drew said while grinning.

Meg shook her head. "No. It was so gross. The worst thing I've ever put in my mouth for sure. I don't like oysters. Not one bit." She pushed the plate away.

Drew laughed, then leaned over and whispered, “You’re adorable when you’re disgusted.”

She playfully slapped at his arm, then took another sip of water hoping to wash away the oyster taste. “So, did you change your name?”

“Huh?” Drew looked perplexed.

“Joey said you weren’t Drew back in the day.”

“Oh, yeah.” He nodded. “I used to go by AJ.”

“AJ?” It came out almost as a squeak.

“Yeah. I’m named Andrew, after my dad. And the J was for junior. I was AJ for years.” He smiled. “I decided when we moved to Austin that I wanted my own name, so I went with Drew. Been Drew ever since.”

“When, exactly, were you at McKamy?” She hoped he’d say different years than she was there, but an eerie gut feeling told her it’d be the same years she attended.

“Let’s see, that’d be about sixteen years ago.”

The blood drained from her face and her heart flailed around inside her chest. *It can’t be true. It can’t. I don’t want to believe it.* A cold sweat erupted on the back of her neck.

“Are you okay?” Shayla said. “You don’t look too good.”

“It’s the oyster. I’m suddenly not feeling well at all.” It seemed like a logical excuse to get out of there before all the walls closed in on her.

“I can take you back to your room,” Drew said.

“No.” It came out more forcefully than she’d intended. “I just need some air.”

Drew scooted his chair back. “I’ll go with you.”

“No. I’ll be fine,” she lied. She didn’t want Drew to go with her anywhere.

She stood and walked as quickly as possible from the dining room, her eyes burning with tears that threatened to fall. She didn’t want to break down in the restaurant, so she held it all in until she reached the outer deck. She rushed over to the handrail and leaned over it in time to vomit over the side. *No, no, no. This can't be true. He can't be AJ.*

"Meg?" Shayla said from behind her. "You must have food poisoning or something."

Meg shook her head violently. "That's not it."

"I told the guys I'd come check on you." Shayla peered at her with wide eyes. "Wow. What is wrong?"

Meg couldn't even find the words to describe the montage of emotions churning inside her.

"Meg. Talk to me," Shayla said, concern evident in her voice.

Meg rubbed her temples, too stunned to even speak. *Drew is AJ? AJ is Drew?* She couldn't quite wrap her mind around this revelation.

Shayla wore a bewildered expression. "Explain what's going on."

Squeezing her lips together to prevent them from quivering, Meg stared out across the ocean. She felt like a horse had kicked her in the chest.

"This is a pretty severe reaction to oysters."

Meg steadied herself against the railing. "I remember him."

Shayla blinked several times as if trying to piece things together. "Drew?"

"Yeah." Meg's mouth felt like it was stuffed with cotton.

"But not in a good way, I'm assuming."

Meg closed her eyes. "Drew—aka AJ—was the boy that tormented me in middle school. That teased me about being fat and made fun of me all the time."

"Are you sure? Maybe you've confused him with someone else." Shayla sounded hopeful.

"No." Meg opened her eyes, then sucked in a ragged breath. "There was something familiar about him, but I couldn't put my finger on it." She had no idea it would turn out to be this. "Someone had told him I had a crush on him or something." She paused for a few moments, all the memories of that awkward time swirling around her mind. With trembling lips, she said, "He nicknamed me Megaton. I can still hear it in my head."

Shayla blew out a breath. "Woah."

"I never saw him again after seventh grade, but his words stayed with me. I wanted to lose weight so I wouldn't always be *Megaton*." She wiped at her eyes. "And the worst part is, he probably doesn't even remember it."

"But he isn't the same person he was in middle school." Shayla reached out and smoothed Meg's hair. "None of us are."

Meg shook her head. "Don't try to make excuses for him. He was so mean to me. So mean. I never thought I'd see him again." She glanced up at the night sky. "I can't believe this."

Shayla wrapped her arm around Meg. "You should talk to him."

Meg sniffled. "No, thanks. I don't want anything to do with him right now."

"Let me—"

"No." Meg held her hand up. "Please don't. Just leave it alone."

"But—"

"I mean it, Shayla." She didn't want Shayla getting involved.

"What am I supposed to tell him?" Shayla studied Meg. "He's going to ask what happened to you and why you ran off."

"Tell him I got really sick." Meg shrugged. At this moment, she didn't care what Shayla told him. "So sick I won't be able to see him the rest of the cruise."

"That sounds totally lame and unbelievable."

"I don't care." Meg felt like she'd been zapped with a stun gun, unable to move or even think straight. The man she was falling for was the boy she hated most. She still couldn't believe it.

Shayla stood. In a tentative voice she asked, "Is it okay if I go back and see Joey and at least let him know I'll be with you tonight?"

"Whatever."

"I'm sorry," Shayla said softly.

Shayla left, and Meg walked numbly back to their room. Once inside, she collapsed on her bed, face first. She wanted to be anywhere but there. She rolled to her side. Of all the men in the entire world she could've met on this cruise, it had to be AJ? The one person who'd teased her and made her feel terrible about herself for years. Of course, he wasn't the only one who had ever called her names, but, over the years, he'd become the symbol for all the rude and cutting remarks she'd endured.

His face, as a young teenager, popped into her head. If only she'd recognized him, she wouldn't be feeling like a knife was lodged in her heart. She knew better than to get involved with any men on this cruise. Why hadn't she listened to herself?

She'd been foolish to think there was something real between her and Drew—AJ. He was probably setting her up for some big heartbreak so he could laugh at her all over again, and she fell right into his trap. Because bullies never change. They're mean and awful right to the core. He was the same person—he was just better at hiding it now.

CHAPTER TEN

Drew stared at the ceiling in his room. He was mystified by what had happened earlier. Meg had disappeared with no explanation. Shayla said that Meg had gotten sick or something, but he knew that wasn't true.

He replayed the evening in his head. He thought they were getting along great and headed for something even better. He even thought they'd see each other after this cruise was over. He'd never opened up about his dream of owning a restaurant and being a chef before. Was that what did it? *Did I scare her off?*

Or was it because he'd kissed her? She hadn't seemed to mind. In fact, she'd kissed him back rather passionately. So, what was it?

Had he done or said something?

"Joey, are you awake?" Drew said into the darkness.

"Yeah," came the groggy reply.

"What do you make of this Meg thing?" He hoped his brother might have some insight.

"She's sick. That's what Shayla said."

"But do you buy that?" Something gnawed at Drew. Something

he couldn't quite describe, but it made him think there was more to her reaction than eating that oyster.

"Yeah. Why not?" Joey yawned.

"Because it doesn't make sense. She suddenly got sick?" Seemed contrived.

"Sometimes it comes on fast." Joey yawned again. "Remember that one time when—"

"No. There's something else, but I don't know what it is." Drew recounted their conversation but came up with nothing.

"What could it be?" Joey asked.

"I have no idea. One second she was warm and cuddled up to me and the next she was gone." He was baffled.

"Maybe being with you made her sick." Joey laughed. "It's a joke, bro."

"Not funny." Drew was in no mood for levity.

"You're really into this woman." Joey sounded surprised.

"Yeah. I am." Drew raked his fingers through his hair. "But I have no idea what's going on with her."

"You should talk to her in the morning." Joey moved around in his bed. "She'll probably be feeling better by then. Those oysters got to her. Stop making it into some big thing."

Drew blew out a breath. Joey was probably right. The oysters could've made her sick and she had to get away quickly. Perhaps he was overreacting and it was simply that she didn't feel well.

But something still troubled him about her quick departure.

CHAPTER ELEVEN

Meg struggled to open her heavy, swollen eyelids. Her thoughts went immediately to the night before. Her past had encroached on her present, twisting and tangling her feelings into a heap, and she didn't know what to do about it.

"You know he's a good guy, Right?" Shayla said, breaking into Meg's private pity party.

"I can't hear you, I'm still sleeping." She didn't want to discuss it.

"He was very perplexed last night."

Meg sighed, because Shayla wasn't going to give up. "What did you say to him?" Even though it happened more than fifteen years ago, AJ had hurt her and Drew couldn't change that. Seeing him again brought the old wounds to the surface and she felt like she was thirteen all over again.

"I told him exactly what you told me to." She could hear a hint of reprimand in Shayla's voice. "He didn't believe me, though." Shayla stood and flicked on the overhead light.

Meg squinted against the harsh brightness that burned her

sensitive eyes. "Why do you say that?" Not that she cared. Except she did. But only a little, tiny bit.

"I could tell by the way he acted."

"Well, I don't want to see him again." Meg rubbed her eyes.

"Are you sure about that?" Shayla said, not hiding her skepticism.

"Yes. I'm sure." What else did Shayla want her to say? That she didn't care he was AJ.

Shayla sat on Meg's bed. "You don't want to talk to him about it?"

Meg sat up in bed. "No." What was the point? "I'm going to stay here in the room until we dock in Galveston."

Shayla gave her a you're-doing-the-wrong-thing kind of look. "So you're going to hide?"

"You call it hiding, but I call it being a businesswoman who's dedicated to her career. I really need to get ready for my launch. You know that. I shouldn't have let myself get sidetracked anyway." Once she was entrenched in her work, she'd forget all about Drew.

"You don't want to go to Nassau?" Shayla stood and walked over to her closet, then opened the door.

"No," Meg said, shaking her head to punctuate her decision.

"And swim with the dolphins?" Shayla said from behind the closet door.

"Nope." She didn't want to do anything but work on her website.

Shayla peeked around the door. "Come on, Meg," she begged. "This is the trip of a lifetime. We're in the Bahamas. And Drew is a good guy who made a mistake when he was a kid." Shayla peered at Meg. "He was what? Twelve or Thirteen?"

"You don't know what it was like." She didn't have to defend herself to Shayla.

"Oh, because you're the only girl who's ever been teased, right?" Shayla put her hand on her hip. "Because I wasn't ever teased. Not because I had an accident in second grade and was called Pee Girl for years. Or for wearing braces. Or because I sent a note to a guy I liked in sixth grade and the mean girls taped it up inside a glass case and everyone saw it. Yeah, didn't live that down for a few years."

"I didn't even know about that stuff," Meg said, suddenly feeling small.

"Because by the time I met you, it was all over. I'd moved on," Shayla said with conviction. "You're losing out on something that could be awesome because you're still mad at him for something he did as a kid."

"Shouldn't you be on my side?" Meg said, miffed at her BFF.

Shayla pointed at her. "I'm on the side of getting you and Drew together."

"That's not going to happen." If Meg was sure of anything, she was sure of this.

Shayla sat by her. "Only because you're hanging onto a grudge."

What was Shayla suggesting? "I should pretend he never hurt me?"

"No." Shayla shook her head. "I didn't say that."

"What then?" As far as Meg was concerned, there weren't any other options.

Shayla patted Meg's hand. "Talk to him about it."

Meg had no desire to see or talk to Drew. No matter what she'd felt for him, knowing he was AJ changed everything. "No."

"I hope you change your mind." Shayla stood and grabbed her beach towel. "Good luck on your website."

"You still aren't going to tell him any of this, right?"

"Nope. I'll just lie to him again and tell him you still aren't feeling well." Shayla's tone didn't leave any doubt that she didn't support Meg in this. At all.

"Thank you."

Shayla gave a quick nod, then shut the door. Meg tried to tamp down the feelings of guilt. She didn't want to make Shayla lie for her, but she didn't see another alternative. And she really did need to work on her site. She picked up her laptop.

After she was sure they were all off the ship, she'd sneak up and get something to eat, then spend the day going through her site. Sounded like the best kind of day. Except her stomach felt queasy. Her throat was thick. And her eyes ached.

A KNOCK SOUNDED at the door, making Meg jump.

Setting her laptop aside, Meg said, "Who is it?"

"It's Drew."

Her heart plummeted to her stomach. *Oh no. What is he doing here?* She obviously couldn't pretend she wasn't in the room. *What to do? What to do?*

After a long pause, she said, "Hi." She intended to keep their interaction short and to the point.

"I wanted to check on you. Shayla said you still aren't feeling well from that oyster last night."

"Yeah," she lied through the door.

"Can I take you to the ship's doctor? Or get you anything?"

"No." She resisted the idea that he was being sweet to check on her.

"Will you open the door at least?" After a momentary pause, he said, "Meg, I know there's something else. Let me in and we'll talk about it."

Meg sat there in silence.

"Meg? Are you going to let me in?" His voice was low.

She still said nothing, because what could she say? It wasn't that she'd thought about his hurtful words every day—or that she'd even thought about them recently—but seeing him dredged up strong emotions and she couldn't reconcile being with him.

A part of her wanted to yell at him and get it all out in the open, but the bigger part of her wanted him to go away so she could regroup.

After several minutes, she looked through the peephole in the door. He was gone. A sense of relief washed over her. *Good. That's the best option*. She'd go her way and he'd go his. End of story.

~

"DID YOU TALK TO HER?" Shayla asked. Drew suspected Shayla knew more than she was letting on.

He wished Meg had opened the door and talked to him. "No." He let out a breath of exasperation.

"Oh." Shayla stiffened.

Drew studied her. "What is going on?" Maybe if he pressured Shayla enough, she'd tell him the truth.

Shayla shrugged, then looked away.

"Please, tell me why she's locked in your room. I know she isn't sick." He desperately wanted to know what had precipitated such a drastic change.

"I have no other information to tell you." Shayla held her hand up.

Drew shook his head. Shayla had answers he needed, but, obviously, she wasn't going to offer any. He wanted to yell in frustration.

"Our excursion is all set," Joey said as he approached them on the deck.

"I'm excited for it," Shayla said.

"I don't think I'll join you." Drew wasn't at all in the mood to go on any excursion.

"What are you going to do?" Joey looked at him.

"Stay here on the ship and maybe swim, read a book. Something." What he really wanted to do was figure out why Meg was avoiding him. Because it was clear that's what was happening.

"Give her some time," Shayla said.

"I knew it. She isn't sick at all. She's mad at me. Or upset. I don't know. One minute we were talking and the next, she was gone. I don't get it." He honestly had no idea what sent her running away from him.

“That’s all I’m going to say.” Shayla gave him a short nod.

“Come with us,” Joey said. “Hanging out here will be boring. At least you can see the beach.”

Even though Drew didn’t feel like going, Joey had a point. He might as well do something with his day. And if he spent enough time with Shayla she’d finally tell him what was going on, wouldn’t she?

CHAPTER TWELVE

After spending an hour or so reading a book about online marketing and how to maximize a website for customer conversions, she applied some changes including fonts and colors. She spent the next hour reading and rereading her copy for search engine optimization keywords and phrases until her eyes were crossed. She started reading another book on website design when her stomach protested and reminded her she hadn't eaten anything. It was probably safe to venture out since everyone had left for the shore excursions. She'd slip into one of the dining areas and grab a bite, then head back to the room to do some more revisions. She hadn't made much progress because thoughts of Drew kept distracting her.

She put on some shorts and a t-shirt, then took the elevator up to the Lido Deck where restaurants surrounded the pool. Since it was lunch time, she had the option of going to the buffet in the dining room. None of the food looked very appetizing, but her stomach screamed for some nourishment.

Grabbing a salad and couple of rolls from the buffet, she found a table toward the back of the restaurant area.

"May I join you?" came a deep, unfamiliar voice from behind her.

She turned and glanced up to see a guy with brown eyes and blonde wavy hair. Before she could say anything, he sat at the table.

"My name is Richard. I'm from Louisiana."

"Hi. I'm Meg from Houston." Was there any way she could leave? She didn't want to carry on a conversation with this guy.

"Nice to meet you, Meg from Houston. Is this your first singles cruise?" He took a sip of his lemonade.

"Yes." If she kept her answers to only one word maybe he'd get the hint and leave.

"Mine too. My mother booked it for me. Told me I needed to find a woman." He smiled, but it had no effect on Meg.

She nodded.

"I'm in finance."

"Awesome." She said it as blandly as possible.

"What do you do?"

This guy wasn't getting the hint. If she told him she was a psychic and there was definitely no future for them, would he leave her alone? She smiled to herself at the idea, but opted to simply tell him the truth. "I'm a nutritionist and a personal trainer. I'm about to launch an online fitness business."

"Cool. I'm into fitness." He showed her his well-defined biceps.

"Fitness is good." Could this conversation be any worse? She shoved a bite of salad into her mouth, hoping she might choke on it and put herself out of her misery.

"My brother runs marathons." He reached over and grabbed one of her rolls. "Said I should give them a try. Maybe you'd be interested in training me?"

He took one of my rolls? That's so rude. "Oh, well, you live in Louisiana and I'm in Houston." *Thank goodness.*

He leaned in and whispered, "For you, I'd be willing to move."

Trying to control the irritation this typical looking-to-hook-up kind of guy created inside her, she said, "Well, I wouldn't want you to do that." Meg looked up and past him and suddenly, her heart stopped beating. There was Drew. Across the dining room. He stood and started walking. *Oh no. He didn't leave the ship. He's coming this way. What should I do?*

Richard followed her line of sight, then said, "Do you have something going on with that guy?"

"No. Nothing. I don't have anything with him. At all." Meg turned her head, hoping Drew wouldn't spot her. "I need to get back to work. In my cabin."

"You're working?" Richard crinkled his nose. "On a cruise?"

Meg used her hand to shield her face. "Yeah. I have a launch date really soon and need to get some more work done."

Drew was approaching. *I need to get out of here. Right now.* Meg's nerves sizzled and her stomach cramped as she tried to figure out what to do. At the last second, Drew disappeared. She let out a sigh of relief.

"Can't you finish your lunch?" Richard asked. "We can get together later."

"No. I don't think so. Have a great time on the cruise." She couldn't make it any clearer than that.

Meg rose. She didn't want to get caught by Drew and have to explain anything to him. She rushed out of the restaurant area and headed to the elevator. Her heart thumped against her ribs while she waited for the elevator doors to open. Once they opened, she jumped inside and hit the button to her floor. Right before the doors closed, someone leaped inside.

It was Drew.

CHAPTER THIRTEEN

Meg swallowed hard. The last person she wanted to be with in a small enclosed space was Drew.

He didn't say anything. After the elevator started to descend, he hit the stop button.

"What are you doing?" Meg demanded.

"You've been avoiding me." He stepped closer to her. "And I want to know why."

Meg sucked in some air. She didn't want to get into this right here or right now.

"I don't understand what's going on. Things were going so well between us." He moved even closer to her, his cologne drawing her in, and she struggled to stay focused. "Please, say something."

What could she say? That he was the boy who'd hurt her and she still carried the grudge? It sounded simple, but it wasn't. His words had affected her and he didn't get a free pass just because they were adults now.

"I'm not going to start this elevator until you talk to me." He crossed his arms in front of his chest.

"Then I guess we'll be here all day." She took a defiant stance.

"What happened? Did I say or do something?" He held his hands out to her. The same hands that had held her close and made her feel things she'd never felt before.

She argued with herself about saying anything. Meg knew he wouldn't be satisfied until she gave him a reason for her sudden change of behavior, so she tried to come up with something but words failed her.

Drew reached up and gently grasped Meg by the shoulders. "Meg, we have the beginning of something great between us."

She peered at him, trying to keep her resolve. "Do we?"

"Yes. Let's not lose it."

Looking into his eyes was too disarming, so she cast her gaze to the floor. She stepped to the side of him, making him drop his hands. She hit the button for her floor. When the doors opened, she turned to him and said, "Are you sure you'd want to be seen with Megaton?" She stepped out of the elevator and kept walking.

Drew watched her walk away, his heartbeat echoing in his ears. *Megaton?* He stepped backwards and fell slightly against the back of the elevator. Memories of middle school circled his head and crashed into his brain. Meg, the woman he'd met on this cruise and fallen for, was the same girl he'd known in middle school? Meg was Megaton? He hadn't thought about that nickname in years.

The elevator doors closed and he stared at them. No wonder she was so upset. She'd been ignoring him since she realized they'd gone to the same middle school and that he used to be called AJ. It all made sense now. Stupid, painful sense.

Meg waited until she was inside her room before she let the angry tears fall. She was angry at Shayla for making her come on this cruise. She was angry at Drew for all the things he'd said to her back in middle school. She was angry at Fate for bringing them together again. And she was angry at herself for falling for him.

She plopped on the bed and let out a long groan. She grabbed the pillow and threw it at the door, wishing it was at his head instead. The more she thought, the more the fire raged in her cheeks and the faster her heart beat. Raw, intense anger replaced her hurt feelings. She wanted to scream at him. Punch him. Tell him where to go.

Grabbing her laptop, she forced herself to bring up her exercise videos so she could edit them. She needed something to divert her thoughts. After a few minutes of pounding the keys on her computer, she said aloud, "I'm so mad, I think I'm going to burst right here."

She tossed her laptop to the side and flicked on the TV inside her room. Maybe she could find something to take her mind off this impossible and ridiculous situation before she blew a gasket.

THE DOOR FLUNG open and Joey walked inside. "Hey, bro."

Drew glanced up from his bed, where he'd spent the last couple hours sprawled out. "Hey. How was Nassau?"

"Great. By far, the best day I've had in a long time." Joey's grin swallowed his face.

Drew sat up. Even though his cruise experience was in shambles, he was relieved that Joey was finally out of his funk—the main reason they'd even come on this trip. At least something had gone right. "Oh yeah?"

Joey pulled the chair out and sat on it. "We had so much fun. Shayla is great. She's so spontaneous and full of interesting ideas. Had me laughing all day. I haven't felt this happy in a long, long time. We really connected."

"Good." Drew tried to push aside the jealousy that flared. He was thrilled that Joey had such a great time, but the resentment stung. He'd planned to spend the day with Meg and add more amazing memories to this trip. Instead, he felt like he'd been trampled by a herd of elephants.

Joey studied him. "What did you end up doing?"

"Not a lot." He shrugged. "I did go to lunch."

"And?" Joey leaned in.

Drew shifted his weight. "I saw Meg."

"Did you say anything to her?"

"I trapped her in the elevator. I was convinced that all I needed was a few minutes to find out what was wrong." He hadn't been prepared for what she said and the memory still felt like his heart had been slashed.

"Did you find out?" Joey asked with wide eyes.

"Yep." Drew's shoulders slumped.

"So, what was it?"

Drew narrowed his eyes. "Shayla didn't tell you?"

"No." Joey shook his head to emphasize his answer. "This is *your* drama, bro."

Drew nodded and adjusted the collar of his shirt. "Remember when we were talking and found out we went to the same middle school?"

"Yeah."

"Turns out we were there at the same time."

"Woah." Joey sat back against the chair. "That's a huge coincidence. But why would that make her want to avoid you?"

Drew cleared his throat.

"She must've remembered what a loser you were back then." Joey started laughing, but sobered up when he saw that Drew didn't even crack a smile. "I don't get it. Why is she mad?"

Drew massaged his temples. "Turns out, I actually knew her."

Joey stared at him. "Really?"

"I thought she was nice." Drew wiped his hands on his shorts. "I mentioned it to one of my friends and he started teasing me that I liked her, then made fun of her because she wasn't . . . skinny."

"She was fat?" Joey seemed surprised.

Drew nodded. "Then someone said she had a crush on me, and the guys gave me such a hard time. They were relentless about it."

"What did you do?"

Casting his gaze to the ground, he said, "What any other seventh grade boy that wanted to be cool would do. I made fun of her to prove them wrong. I even made up a name for her. *Megaton.* And it caught on." He glanced up at Joey. "Then we moved and I lost contact with all those people. I knew I'd been a jerk to her, but I brushed it off. You know, because I was so mature and all. It was stupid middle school stuff."

"That was years ago."

"Yes, but she's still hurt about it. Or she wouldn't have reacted the way she did." As a kid he didn't think his words would have so much power. Now, as an adult and after examining his relationship with his dad, he could see the harm words could do.

Joey wrinkled his forehead. "What are you going to do about it?"

"I don't know. How do you make up for something like that to someone?" He couldn't call the words back and he couldn't erase the damage he'd caused.

CHAPTER FOURTEEN

Meg startled when the door opened. She hadn't realized that she'd fallen asleep.

"Sorry, I didn't mean to wake you," Shayla said, stepping inside.

"No worries." Meg rubbed her eyes. "How was everything today?"

Shayla sat on the bed next to Meg. She covered her mouth, but Meg could see a smile peeking out between her fingers. "What?" Meg asked as she sat up and stared at Shayla.

"I think I'm in love." Shayla giggled.

"Again?" Shayla fell in love about as often as she did laundry.

With a serious expression, Shayla said, "For real this time."

"Really?" Meg tried to keep the suspicious tone out of her voice.

"Yes. I know, I know." She held up her hands. "I seem to fall in love easily, I know. But this is different."

"How so?" Meg asked, doubtful but still intrigued.

"Joey is kind and thoughtful. He's funny. We talk a lot. He makes me feel good. I want to spend all my time with him. And," she paused, "I could see myself building a life with him."

Meg sat there dumbfounded. Shayla had never said *that* before. "Wow."

"See? This *is* different." Shayla gave a contented smile.

"Maybe you're right." It didn't seem super likely that she'd find someone worth dating beyond this cruise—especially someone with a brother like AJ—but Meg couldn't ignore the way Shayla's eyes lit up as she talked about Joey.

"Say it." Shayla stared at her.

"What?"

"I know there's lots going on up there." She pointed at Meg's head. "Just tell me."

"If you've found something great, then I'm glad. Really." She was happy for Shayla, despite her own misery.

Shayla cocked her head at Meg. "But?"

"No but." She didn't want to spoil Shayla's enthusiasm with her own negativity and doubts.

"Yes, there's a but."

"No there—"

"Meg." Shayla said it in such a way that Meg knew she'd have to say what was on her mind.

"Fine." She tried to think how to say it delicately. "This ship is full of losers." Meg had met most of them personally, and AJ was at the top of that list.

Shayla visibly stiffened. "Joey is not one of them."

"Maybe not. But how well do you actually know him?"

"Like was he mean in middle school?" Shayla said it with an edge to her voice.

Meg gave her a sharp look.

"Sorry. That wasn't fair." Shayla reached her arm around Meg. "I just want you to understand that I really, really, really like him."

Unfortunately, Meg could understand that all too well—that was the problem. She really, really, really liked a man she couldn't stand.

"I'm so sorry about everything with Drew, and I know you're

hurt, but you can't hold Joey responsible for what his brother did. Joey is wonderful, and I want to spend more time with him."

Meg didn't want to dampen Shayla's excitement. Her best friend deserved to be happy. If, against all odds, she found a good man on this cruise, then she should explore that. And she was right, Joey shouldn't be penalized for his brother's actions. "Then you should spend time with him."

"But that means you may have to see Drew," Shayla said softly.

Every muscle in Meg's body tensed at the thought of having to spend any time with AJ, even if he now called himself Drew.

"Like dinner tonight." Shayla gave a weak smile.

"Uh, no, thanks." She couldn't think of a worse way to spend her evening.

Shayla stood and walked over to her closet. "You have to eat."

"Not with him." Meg would rather starve.

Shayla turned and peered at Meg. "Before you knew he was that kid from middle school, you were totally falling for him. Like seriously falling."

"Yeah, don't remind me." Meg wanted to forget this whole cruise ever happened.

Taking a few steps toward her, Shayla reached out her hands and said, "Can't you forget he was that kid?"

Meg jerked her head back in indignation. "Are you kidding me?"

"But it was so long ago. And you are so miserable right now. If you'd only forgive and forget—"

"I *know* it was a long time ago. I know I'm holding a grudge from middle school, but you don't know how he bullied me. All because of my big sin of being overweight." Saying the words made her cheeks heat up and her anger start to sizzle again.

Shayla sat next to her and wrapped her arm around Meg's shoulder. "Now might be the perfect time to get rid of all that baggage. Throw it away. Throw away AJ."

Finally, Shayla gets it. "That's what I've been saying."

"No." Shayla shook her head. "That isn't what I meant. Throw away AJ and all those memories, but let Drew in."

"I can't do that." Allowing him into her life now would be like pretending nothing ever happened. It'd be like condoning what he did.

Shayla squeezed Meg's shoulder. "You *can* do it. One step at a time."

Meg shook her head. No way was she going to forget what happened. No way.

"Start with dinner," Shayla said in a hopeful tone.

The idea of sitting down to dinner as if everything was fine was ludicrous. "No. You go ahead."

"But—"

"Really, Shayla. I don't want to be a downer for you and Joey. Go enjoy tonight together. I'll get something to eat later."

"I wish you'd change your mind." Shayla stood and walked over to the bathroom.

After Shayla left for dinner, Meg refused to think any more about AJ—Drew. She turned her attention to her website where she'd edited her videos and uploaded her meal plans. She planned to give away a week's worth of menus to help draw traffic to her site. Clicking on the About tab, she reread her bio and added another paragraph about her plans and what she wanted to do with her site. If all went well, she'd quit her day job at Better Life and focus solely on her online business.

She checked her phone and was surprised to see a couple of hours had passed. A stray thought of Drew flashed across her mind and she let it linger wondering what tonight might have been like between them. She absently touched her lips, then said aloud, "No. Stop thinking about him. Nothing will ever happen between us."

With a loud roar of her stomach, she shut her laptop and left the room hoping to find food somewhere. When she finally found some pizza, she didn't dare sit at any table and alert all the losers on deck that she was there. Taking her pieces of pizza in a napkin, Meg went back to her room.

Once she caught the sight of her door, the memory of the note from Drew that had made her heart flutter, now only made anger bubble to the surface.

How dare he trick me into liking him.

Just when she thought she'd found someone, he ended up being the poster boy for Most Wanted Jerk. She opened the door and slammed it behind her.

CHAPTER FIFTEEN

Drew lay in bed, a million thoughts darting through his mind. He'd missed Meg at dinner, but he didn't blame her for not coming. He wished she could expunge the memory of him as a thoughtless teenager and see him as an adult. Not that he was perfect by any means, but he wasn't the same person he once was. If only Meg could see that.

He rolled to his side. This whole thing was so frustrating because he'd never felt this way before. He'd dated plenty of women over the years, but none had held him captive the way Meg had in only a few days. He still couldn't believe he'd felt so much in so little time. Too bad it couldn't go anywhere. Or could it?

Could he reason with her and ask for her forgiveness? For another chance? Should he? He moved to his other side.

The door opened and Joey entered the dark cabin.

"I'm awake," Drew said.

"Oh." Joey flipped on the light and Drew squinted against it.

"I can't believe we only have one more day left." He shut the door behind him. "This has been the greatest week."

"You're planning to see Shayla after the cruise?" Drew asked, already knowing the answer.

"Of course." Joey grinned. "We've made plans for next weekend. I'm going to Houston to see her."

"I'm glad." He meant it. The whole point of this cruise was to help Joey live his life again and that seemed to have happened. So it was all good, even if things didn't work out with Meg the way he wanted them to.

"And you'll come with me to Houston?" Joey sat on his bed across from Drew.

"Nah." What would be the point?

"Maybe after Meg has a little time, she won't be so mad."

Drew wished that would be true, but he didn't hold out much hope. "I don't think so."

Joey took off his shoes. "What are you gonna do if me and Shayla get serious?"

"Be happy for you." What was Joey driving at?

"No. I mean if we get *really* serious."

Drew sat up, then knit his brows together. "What are you saying?"

"I think I'm in love with her and I might . . . well . . . maybe . . ."

"What?" Drew studied his brother. "You aren't talking about marrying her."

With a shrug, Joey said, "Why not?"

"Because you hardly know her. You've only known her for a few days." Marriage shouldn't be taken lightly.

"Is there a time requirement on when you can decide if you want to marry someone?" Joey took off his shirt and tossed it on the floor.

"I wanted to get you out of your bad mood, not marry you off to someone you just met."

Joey peered at him. "Tell me you don't have strong feelings for Meg."

Drew shifted his weight. "We aren't talking about me."

"We are now." Joey threw his pants on the floor and slid into his bed. "You've fallen for her. Hard."

"Doesn't matter anymore." Sadness and frustration set into the pit of his stomach.

Joey jumped up, flicked off the light, and got back into the bed. "Why?"

"Because she's made it pretty clear she doesn't want to see me again." No matter how much he wished it were different, it wasn't.

"Since when do you ever back down from a challenge? You go after what you want and what you think is right every day at work." Joey said it so matter-of-factly.

"This is different." Drew adjusted the uncomfortable pillow under his head.

"Maybe, but the principle is the same."

"If I thought—"

"What?" Joey said, cutting Drew off. "If she felt the same about you? Of course she does."

Drew rose up on an elbow, a ribbon of hope rushing through him. "Did Shayla say that?"

"Well, no. But it's obvious. She wouldn't have gotten so mad if she didn't have deep feelings."

Drew collapsed back down on his too-hard bed. "They're only deep feelings because of all the things I said to her back in school." He wanted to call back every harsh word he'd said.

Joey made some noise as he shifted in his bed. "I think she cares about you as much as you care about her. And I'm betting she's been miserable, too."

"But I can't force her to give me another chance. I can't make her want to be with me." He kicked off his blanket.

"You can go talk to her." It sounded like such a simple solution coming from Joey.

"Except she won't talk to me."

"She isn't totally unreasonable. She's hurt. Tell her how you feel. Tell her how sorry you are for everything you said back in the day."

Drew blew out a big puff of air. "Do you think she'd listen?"

"Yeah," Joey said with conviction.

Drew wasn't as convinced.

CHAPTER SIXTEEN

When Meg awoke the next morning, she was alone in her room. Though she was sincerely glad that Shayla had found someone, she wished that someone didn't have a rat for an older brother.

She sat up in bed and turned on her laptop to check over her website again. She loaded each video to make sure every one of them ran properly. Watching herself doing exercises on-screen wasn't her favorite, but she hoped that women would find them appealing and easy enough to follow. The website looked good and everything seemed to be working the way that it should, which pleased her. All her hard work was about to pay off. This was a time to celebrate and bask in her accomplishment.

So why was celebrating so disheartening?

The answer was simple, but the solution wasn't. Meg realized she was holding a long-time grudge, but the memories made her feel like they happened only yesterday. In a million, trillion years she didn't think she'd ever come face-to-face with her nemesis, AJ. And to have him wrapped up as Drew was almost too much. She'd harbored these angry feelings for so long, she wasn't sure how to let them go. Or if she even wanted to let them go. But her feelings for Drew were strong—stronger than she wanted to admit.

She felt like a ping pong ball with her emotions bouncing all over the place. While caught up in her thoughts, her stomach reminded her that she hadn't eaten. Did she dare leave her room?

Maybe some sunshine and sea air would do her some good. The odds that she'd run into Drew were probably low enough that she could slip into the dining area without notice. She'd wear her sunglasses and her best leave-me-alone-and-don't-talk-to-me expression to dissuade any of the single men from approaching her. In less than twenty-four hours she'd finally be off this getting-smaller-by-the-minute boat and could focus on her real life.

JOEY WAS OFF WITH SHAYLA, so Drew was left to himself. He'd tossed over his conversation with Joey and had decided he'd try to find Meg and talk to her. Realizing she might refuse, he vowed he'd try anyway.

In the bathroom off the Lido Deck, Drew adjusted his shirt and gazed at himself in the mirror trying to muster up as much courage as possible. He could simply walk away and never look back. He could accept that he and Meg weren't meant to be together and go on with his life as if he'd never felt the way he did.

He shook his head. That's not what he wanted.

The door opened and a guy about his age with a receding hairline walked in. "Having any luck?"

"Luck?"

"With the ladies," the guy sang out.

"Oh."

"I've got less than a day to find me a woman." He checked his teeth in the mirror.

Drew nodded, unsure what else to say.

"I've approached so many women. I don't believe in small talk, you know." He smoothed the hair on the side of his head. "I get right to the point."

"Has that worked?"

The guy's shoulders slumped. "Not yet."

Drew was the last one to give any advice on relationships, but he wanted to offer this guy some hope. "Is it time to rethink your strategy?"

Shrugging, the balding man said, "Why is it so hard?"

"You got me," Drew said, knowing exactly what the guy meant.

As he left the bathroom, Drew started to rethink his own strategy. Maybe it was a bad idea to find Meg. She'd made it crystal clear that she wanted nothing to do with him. Why was he wasting his time? What was done was done, and there was no going back. Right?

He started walking toward the Lido Deck. As he rounded the corner near the elevator, he ran right into Joey and Shayla.

"Look who it is," Joey said, his arm around Shayla. "Where have you been?"

"In the bathroom."

"All morning?" Joey wrinkled his forehead.

Drew gave him a look. "No, just now. Before that, I was in our room."

"He's been no fun ever since, you know," Joey said to Shayla.

"Same," Shayla said.

"What?" Drew looked between them.

"Nothing." Shayla snuggled up to Joey.

Over the intercom a deep voice said, "This is Matteo, your friendly cruise director. Have you been having a good time? Yeah, you have. But it's not over yet. Come out on the Lido Deck by the pool. We've saved the best for last. It's time for . . . wait for it . . . the hairiest chest contest. You know you want to come. Hurry. Right now."

Shayla made a face. "Ew."

"It'd be funny," Joey said. "We should go watch it. Maybe you should enter, Drew." He laughed.

"No, thanks. I'm going back to—"

"This is the last day. Don't spend it in the room, man." Joey punched Drew in the arm.

"Come hang out with us," Shayla insisted.

Though going to the room sounded appealing, Drew didn't want to hang out down there by himself. *Might as well watch this contest.* "All right."

They walked over to the deck where a crowd had already gathered. Drew was sure to not make eye contact with any of the women. He had no desire to talk to any of them. Except for Meg. He still wanted to see her and try to make things right. He shook his head. *Stop thinking about her.*

"We've got our participants. Now we need some female volunteers," Matteo said.

Some women at the front of the crowd raised their hands and Matteo chose a couple of them.

"This should be interesting," Joey said.

"Ladies," Matteo said, "you will be our judges."

A woman with short red hair smiled. The woman next to her, with curly brown hair and wearing a bikini, clapped her hands together. Five men stood to the side, all wearing t-shirts.

The woman with red hair said with a southern drawl, "How do we judge?"

"I'm glad you asked." Matteo smiled. He cleared his throat, then said, "This is how it goes. The men over here will remove their shirts. You will then run your fingers through their hairy chest to get an idea of the fullness. The guy with the most hair wins."

Shayla leaned in. "I would hate it if I were one of those girls. So. Much. Ew."

Joey laughed. "This will be great."

"If you say so," Drew said. He resisted the urge to scan the deck for Meg.

CHAPTER SEVENTEEN

Meg finished her shrimp salad and sat back. She could hear some commotion coming from the pool deck, so she decided to check it out on the way back to her room.

As she neared the area, she could see men with their shirts off. Very hairy men. And some poor woman was running her hands all over one of the men's chests. Another one of the guys flexed his hairy pecs several times and a few women squealed.

A short woman next to her said, "I love a man with a hairy chest. Very masculine."

Meg nodded. "If that's what you like."

"I do. I do." The woman turned to her. "Have you enjoyed the cruise?"

"I'm anxious to get home."

"Didn't meet anyone?"

Meg shrugged. What could she say? That she'd met someone who took her breath away, made her giddy, and turned her heart into mush, only to find out he'd been the boy who'd bullied her in middle school? Sounded preposterous.

"I met a cute guy a couple of days ago. Turns out he wears

women's lingerie on the weekends for fun. Not my thing, you know?" The woman laughed.

"I'm not sure how I'd react to that."

"Now, there's a hot guy over there." The woman pointed and Meg followed the line of sight right to . . . Drew, of all people.

And worse, Drew saw her at the same moment and their gazes locked on each other. He smiled, then started in her direction, making her heart jump into her throat.

"Uh, I need to go. I hope you find a hairy guy." Meg turned and rushed away.

Before she made it very far, Drew called out, "Meg. Can we talk?"

Against her better judgment, she turned and looked directly at him. His still mesmerizing eyes lured her in like a hummingbird to sugar water. She shook her head to free herself from the pull of his gaze. "I don't think we have anything to talk about."

"I think we do." His expression pleaded with her. "Please."

"I have nothing to say to you." Seeing him brought back all the memories of middle school. Her anger and frustration boiled up again.

He stepped toward her. "I want to say something to you."

She retreated and said, "What if I don't want to hear it?" What could he possibly say to her?

Drew clenched his jaw. "You are maddening."

"*I* am?" Her heartbeat throbbed in her cheeks. "Are you serious?"

"Yes. I want to talk to you but you keep avoiding me."

"Because I don't want to talk to you." She wanted to let all her aggression out. "I . . . I . . . I want to punch you."

"Really?" He gave her a half-smile, as if he didn't believe her, which only fanned the flames of her fury.

"Yeah. Really," she shouted, not caring that a crowd had started forming around them.

Drew held his arms out. "Give me your best shot."

She eyed him. Was he serious? With the most authoritative tone she could muster, she said, "I will."

"Go for it." He dipped his head toward her.

"What?" She took a bold stance. "You don't believe me?"

"I—"

"Because I can tell you, AJ or Drew or whatever you want to call yourself, that I've fantasized about punching you for a long time." She noticed a larger crowd had gathered, but she was too riled up to worry about it.

"You give it to him, honey," a woman with short black hair said.

"We shouldn't be encouraging violence," a tall woman said. "They should talk this through."

"No way. He deserves it," a petite woman with blond hair said.

"Why? Because he's a man?" A bald guy with a goatee said.

"Yeah," the woman with blond hair said. "He's done her wrong."

A skinny guy with a big nose said, "You don't even know what this is about."

"I'll tell you what it's about," Meg yelled over the crowd, rolling her shoulders back and standing straight.

"You tell us, honey."

Meg faced the crowd. "I met him here on this cruise. He was funny. Interesting. Kind. And, you know, obviously good-looking." A group of women nodded their agreement. "We spent the day together in Key West. And Freeport. We swam in the ocean. Gazed at the night sky. Danced. Talked about our dreams." She paused. "Long story short, he made me fall for him."

The women looked at each other. "So?" the black-haired woman said. "That's a problem most of us wish we had." She laughed.

"No, no, no. You don't understand," Meg said, holding her hands up in front of her. "I knew him before." She stepped closer to Drew, folded her arms, and jutted her chin out. "He made fun of me for being fat." She emphasized the last word.

"Oh, that's low, mister," a woman with a flower tattoo on her shoulder said.

A man with a protruding belly said, "I don't get it. You're thin and beautiful." He scratched his head.

"It was when we were in middle school," Meg said.

"Middle school?" the woman with blond hair said, crinkling her nose. "Like when you were kids?"

"Yes." Meg wanted everyone to back her up.

The woman with black hair leaned in and asked, "That was a long time ago. Is he still mean and rude?"

Meg cleared her throat. "Well, no, but—"

"But what?" the woman asked.

"He was really terrible to me." Meg desperately wanted to make everyone understand how she felt.

"I feel awful about how I treated her back then. I want to make it up to her," Drew said.

"Give him another chance, honey."

Meg surveyed the crowd. They all seemed to turn against her. "Wait a minute. You're giving him a get-out-of-jail-free card after all the things he said to me? My name is Meg but he nicknamed me Megaton." She emphasized the last syllable.

"Ohhh, that's a cruel name." A woman with large hoop earrings pointed at Drew.

"You're right it is." Meg could feel the tide turning in her favor.

"I agree wholeheartedly," Drew said to the crowd. "It was very cruel and there was no excuse. I wasn't strong enough to stand up to my friends. I'd told one of my buddies that I thought she was nice. He immediately started laughing and making fun of me. Instead of standing up to him, I joined in and went that extra mile to fit in with my friends."

"That's legitimate," the skinny guy said.

"No, it isn't." Meg couldn't believe how wishy-washy these people were. "Because his friend was rude and mean, he can do the same?"

"I'm not proud of how I acted, and I wish I could change the past. But I can't. And I don't want to lose my future because of it."

"Aww, give him a chance," the tall woman said.

“I think *I’m* in love with him,” said an Asian woman who was fanning herself.

Drew peered directly at Meg, and her breath caught. “I’m going to keep proving to you that I’ve changed and that I want you in my life.”

“Come on, honey, kiss and make up. Don’t lose this great guy.”

Meg wanted to scream. “I don’t know what is wrong with all of you. This whole thing is ridiculous and I’m done.” Meg hated that this had turned into such a spectacle.

“Does that mean you aren’t going to punch him?” said the bald guy.

Meg let out a frustrated breath and stepped through the crowd without looking back.

“I meant what I said,” Drew called after her.

CHAPTER EIGHTEEN

Back in the room, Meg fumed. She wasn't sure if she was angrier with Drew or with the stupid people who were on his side. What a completely ludicrous thing.

Shayla opened the door and stepped inside. "Wow, that was quite the—"

"Don't. Even. Say. It." Meg was even more eager to get off this boat.

Plopping on the chair, Shayla said, "You have to give him credit for—"

"Credit? Everyone is acting like I'm way off here. I'm not. He hurt me." Why was this so hard to grasp?

"And he's apologized. What else do you want?"

"Nothing. I want nothing from him." Meg pulled at her hair. "Actually, what I want is for this trip to be over and done."

Shayla shook her head.

"What?" Meg blinked several times.

With a smirk, Shayla said, "It's so obvious that the two of you are in love."

"In love? Are you crazy? I'm not in love with him. I'm not even in like with him. I never want to see him again. Ever. I wish I'd never met him. My life would be so much better if I'd never come on this cruise," Meg protested.

"Uh huh." Shayla crossed her legs. "I can tell."

Meg did not want to have this conversation with Shayla. "Don't you need to go see Joey or something?"

"Yeah, but I want you to come with me. We can hang out and—"

"No, thanks. I'm going to finish up some work, then take a shower and pack all my stuff so I can be ready to get off this ship ASAP in the morning." *The sooner, the better.*

Shayla stood. "I'll be back before dinner."

After Shayla left, Meg stared at the door. Now that the adrenaline in her system had started to slow, she was left feeling embarrassed that so many people had witnessed her semi-breakdown. She hadn't planned for that to happen or for it to be public. A part of her still wanted to punch Drew, but another part of her wanted to run away with him and forget everything else. *Stop it. Right now. No wanting to run away with him.*

Meg needed to get back home—back to her normal, everyday life—and get on with her plans. Meeting Drew had thrown her off-balance. Finding out he was AJ completely knocked her down. Once she was home, she could put this cruise in perspective and sort through all her mishmashed feelings to find her balance again. This trip would be a distant memory.

AFTER TAKING A SHOWER, Meg spent time proofreading the copy on her website, playing around with the settings, and testing the subscription links. She also designed some images she could use as ads for her site. Most of the work was done, but she didn't dare go out of her room because she didn't want to risk seeing Drew again and lose her resolve. Thankfully, he hadn't come by to try to see her. A teeny, tiny part of her was disappointed by that, but she swept it aside.

When a knock sounded, Meg checked the peephole to see who it was. She opened the door to a cruise employee.

"Yes?" She hoped there wasn't a problem.

"I have a delivery for you," the man with the mustache said.

"You do?" She blinked.

He handed her a vase of red roses.

"Uh, thank you."

She didn't have to guess who they were from. Her first impulse was to dump them in the trash. Instead, she set the flowers on the small table and stared at them, unwilling to read the card. Finally, she couldn't stand it anymore.

On the card, Drew had written, "Meg, I truly am sorry. Let's start over."

She shook her head. Did he expect that a few flowers would make up for everything?

Shayla opened the door and breezed in. "Oh, are these from Drew?" She made a loud inhaling sound.

"As if you don't already know the answer. You probably put him up to it." It wouldn't surprise her if Shayla was conspiring with Drew.

"Nope." She set her purse down. "I've been with Joey at the casino. Haven't seen Drew since, you know, your big show."

"Don't remind me." The back of her neck heated at the memory.

Shayla opened her closet. "This is the last night on the cruise. Don't you want to come out and enjoy it?" She pulled out a red floral print dress and put it on.

"I've had as much of this cruise as I can take." All Meg wanted to do was sleep away the rest of the cruise—it'd go by faster that way.

"You're gonna sit in here and do nothing all night?" Shayla made it sound so dreadful.

Meg shrugged. "What do you want me to say?"

"That Drew is a great guy. That the two of you have something awesome. That you want to explore it and see where it goes." Shayla held a hand out. "You know, something like that."

"I'm not sure how else to explain this to you, but his words have rolled around my head for years. I can't ignore that." Meg was tired of explaining herself over and over and over again.

"I get it. I do. And what he said and did back then was wrong—completely wrong. But he's not the same person," Shayla said with passion. "Don't you see that?"

Meg didn't say anything.

"You want to be bitter about this the rest of your life?" Shayla peered at her with intensity. "Be miserable about it for forever?"

"No. Of course not." That's not what she was doing. Was it?

"You have the power, Meg. *You* can decide to let go of this." Shayla pointed at her. "You're a fool for walking away from him. And it's such a waste of time to hold on to all this anger. Besides, you should thank him."

Meg blinked. "Thank him? For what?"

"For making you alive again." Shayla dragged a brush through her hair.

"What are you talking about?" Meg said.

With a hand on her hip, Shayla said, "You've been practically dead emotionally for so long."

"Where is this coming from?" Meg frowned.

"A place of love." Shayla sat on the bed next to Meg. "I've watched you shut yourself off from love for a long time. On this cruise, I finally saw you open up—"

"And what did that get me?"

"Right now?" Shayla patted her hand. "Misery."

"Exactly." Meg simply wanted the heartache to go away.

Shayla raised her eyebrows. "Your fault."

"*My* fault? Are you seriously blaming me for this?" Shayla's assertion insulted Meg. None of this was her fault. At all.

"Someone has to get you to see this for what it is."

Meg shook her head. She wasn't going to shoulder any blame for how Drew had treated her years ago. "You're wrong. Totally wrong."

"No, Meg, you are," Shayla said with fervor. She stood, grabbed her purse, and walked out the door.

Meg gritted her teeth, her blood boiling. How dare Shayla blame her. This was not her fault. She wanted to scream at the top of her lungs at the impossibility of this situation.

A minute or so later, a knock sounded again and Meg angrily opened the door.

"Oh. I'm sorry to bother you. This is for you," a woman dressed in a white uniform said. She handed Meg a box.

"Thanks." Meg shut the door, her feelings all jumbled and snarled together.

Holding the box in her hands, she couldn't decide what to do. It was obviously another gift from Drew. She didn't want it. Well, mostly she didn't. If he thought he was going to win her over with some silly gift or two, he was mistaken.

After another minute or so, she opened it. "Chocolates." Her stomach immediately reacted, so she slipped one of the chocolates into her mouth. The smooth sweetness slid over her tongue. It was delicious. But she wasn't going to let some candy influence her, because this didn't change anything. Really. It didn't.

She noticed the card. Picking it up, she read, "Please give me another chance."

"He's nothing, if not persistent." She pursed her lips so a smile wouldn't tumble out.

CHAPTER NINETEEN

Drew sat near the buffet area drumming his fingers on the table. He saw Shayla and Joey and waved them over. Disappointment settled over him when he realized Meg wasn't with them. Not that he'd expected her to come, but a minute part of him thought she might. He had no idea how she'd reacted to the roses. Or to the chocolates. His stomach was in knots.

"Pretty smooth," Shayla said as she sat.

"I'm sorry." Drew gazed at her.

Shayla touched him on the arm. "Sending Meg those beautiful roses."

"Did she like them?" He straightened, eager to hear what she would say.

"Well, she wouldn't admit she liked them, but I could see it in her eyes." Shayla leaned in. "What's your plan?"

"I don't have one. Just thought I'd send her some gifts to keep her thinking about me, I guess."

"Oh, she will most definitely do that." Shayla laughed.

"Because she's still so mad?" He'd never met a woman who could get so fired up—something he found quite attractive. He only wished it wasn't directed at him.

"Oh, yeah." Shayla wrinkled her forehead. "But that's good."

"It is?" He perked up.

Shayla patted his arm. "Proves she has strong feelings for you."

"But I want strong *positive* feelings." He wiped his hands on his pants.

"I'm sure those are there too," Shayla said with confidence.

"She's got it as bad as you, bro," Joey said. He laughed.

"It'd be a lot easier if I could walk away from her and forget about all this." If only that were a real possibility.

"But you can't." Shayla smiled.

"Nope. I feel like I need to make up for being such a horrible kid. I know I can't totally make up for it, but I want her to know that I'd never mistreat her now. I wish she could forgive me." Meg had done in a few days what other women hadn't done in months—capture his heart.

Shayla reached her arm around Joey and rested her head on his shoulder. "Meg doesn't easily forgive. She likes to hang onto grudges."

"Obviously." He probably knew that better than anyone right now.

"But I also know this." Shayla's head popped up. "She's fallen for you pretty hard. Harder than I've seen her fall for anyone."

"Why is she being so difficult then?" Joey asked. "Women make no sense."

Shayla playfully slapped at Joey's arm. "We totally make sense. Let me explain it to you." Shayla leaned in. "Meg had buried her hurt feelings for a long time. When she found out Drew was AJ, it brought them all rushing back to the surface. Now she's confused and hurt all over again. And trying to figure out her feelings." Shayla smiled. "Makes perfect sense. Also, I know this because I've studied psychology."

"Well, then, Dr. Shayla," Drew said, running his fingers through his hair, "you think she'll come around?"

Shayla nodded.

CHAPTER
TWENTY

When Meg opened her eyes, she realized she'd fallen asleep before Shayla came back to the room last night. She glanced over at Shayla's unmade bed, but Shayla wasn't there. Meg sat up.

Finally, this cruise was coming to an end. As soon as she dressed and packed up her toiletries, she could get in line to get off this boat and never look back. Because that's what she planned to do. Never look back. Or think about Drew again.

The door flew open. "Good morning," Shayla said. "Isn't it a glorious day?" She stepped inside with a grin.

"I'm guessing things went well last night with Joey." Meg swung her legs out of bed and rested her elbows on her knees.

"Yes, yes, and yes. He is so great." Shayla twirled around.

Meg yawned. "I'm glad. Really. I hope things work out for the two of you. Didn't think you'd find anyone like him on this cruise of losers. But I'm happy to be wrong."

Shayla gave her a pointed look. "Are you?"

"About you." Meg held her hand up. "Not anything else."

Shayla planted herself on the bed next to Meg. "Come on, Meg. Don't leave this cruise without talking to Drew."

"I have nothing to say to him." Meg stood and stepped over to the closet. Over her shoulder she said, "And I don't want to discuss it anymore." She had already said everything she wanted to and was done—completely done. She turned and looked at Shayla. "I mean it."

"But what about the flowers?" Shayla pointed to the box of chocolates. "And those?"

"He sent me a couple impersonal gifts." She shrugged one shoulder. "So what?" Some roses—though they were beautiful—and some chocolates—though they were delicious—didn't suddenly make everything better.

Shayla let out a long, audible sigh and fell across the bed. "I give up."

"Good." Meg grabbed her suitcase. "I'll change and pack up the rest of my things so we can get out of here."

"Whatever you say."

Meg brushed her teeth. In a little while they'd be back on the road toward Houston and none of this would matter. She could forget about all of it and get back to her normal life, which is exactly what she intended to do.

After she dressed, Meg put the final things in her suitcase and looked over the room to make sure she wasn't leaving anything. "Are you ready?" she said.

"I think so. I'm meeting Joey out by the elevators on deck four." Shayla grabbed her suitcase. "Do you want to skip that?"

"No. It's fine. It's not like I want Drew to suffer some horrendous fate, you know. I just don't want to date him." Even as the words came out of her mouth, her muscles tensed at the anticipation of seeing him.

They walked down the hall and took the elevator to deck four while Meg's heart rumbled in her chest. She was set in her decision and had no plans to waffle—even when the doors opened and Drew stood there.

Shayla stepped out of the elevator and Meg followed, her breathing shallow.

"Hi," Drew said.

"Hi."

"Can I help you with your suitcase?" He held out his hand.

"I've got it. Thanks." She didn't want to be rude, but she didn't need Drew's help with her suitcase or anything else.

She watched as Shayla threw her arms around Joey and they embraced. "I'm going to miss you," he said.

Shayla gave him a kiss. "We'll see each other in less than a week."

"That's too long to wait." He laughed.

A cloud of awkwardness hung over Meg and Drew. Unsure of what to say, Meg hefted her suitcase and started walking. Seeing Joey and Shayla together made her feel things she didn't want to feel—things like regret and insecurity. Maybe she'd been too rash in her decision to abandon her blossoming relationship with Drew. Maybe she was holding onto a grudge that didn't matter anymore. She shook her head and sent those fleeting thoughts away.

Drew caught up with her. "I have something for you." He held out a box.

Unwilling to take it, she said, "I don't think—"

"Please. I bought it for you." He cast a glance downwards, then back at her. "Before."

Reluctantly, she took the box. Her feelings were so topsy-turvy she felt dizzy. Having Drew so near made her think things she shouldn't think and feel things she didn't want to feel.

"Open it," he said expectantly.

Inside the box was the silver bracelet with a dangly charm inscribed with Key West that she'd admired in the shop during their visit. Memories of that day crashed in on her. "I don't know what to say."

Drew moved in closer, making her heart trip all over itself. "I'm not excusing what I did, or making light of how you felt, but isn't there any way we can move past this? I want to make it up to you." He leaned in and a whiff of his musky cologne wafted past her nose. "I've never felt like this before, and I know you feel something for me too."

She kept her lips pressed together and her mind set.

He scooted even closer, his face only inches from hers. "Tell me you don't feel a connection between us, and I'll leave you alone."

Meg worked her jaw and mustered up all her strength. Casting her gaze at her feet, she said, "I don't."

He reached out and tugged her chin up. "Look at me when you say that."

Resisting the urge to wrap her arms around him and lose herself in his kisses, she looked directly at him and said, "I don't feel a connection." It was the biggest lie she'd ever told.

Drew let his hand fall. "I don't believe you."

"It's the truth," she insisted.

He rubbed his forehead. "I think we have something worth fighting for, but I can't fight for it alone."

"I'm sorry," Meg said, wishing she could wave a magic wand and make the past disappear.

"So am I." Drew stepped back "I apologize again for what I put you through. It was never my intention to hurt you, and I hope someday you can forgive me."

She nodded slightly, then started walking.

"Good luck with your fitness business," Drew called after her.

She stopped and turned around. "Thank you. Good luck with your . . . life."

He gave a small wave.

Meg whirled around and walked briskly away, convincing herself that there was no future for them.

~

MEG WAITED by the shuttle stop anxious to get back to the car and go home. *Where is Shayla? How long can it take to say goodbye?*

After a few minutes, she spotted her best friend and waved her over.

"It's going to take forever to get through this week," Shayla said, leaning against a pole.

"You really have it bad." Meg moved her suitcase closer to her and sat on it.

"So do you." Shayla pointed at her. "You just won't admit it."

Meg said nothing.

When the shuttle arrived, they found their seats. Within ten minutes, they were at the parking lot and twenty minutes later they were in Shayla's car on the freeway headed north.

"I can't wait to get back home." Attempting to keep her mind off the cruise, Meg made mental notes of all the things she needed to accomplish.

"Back to reality," Shayla said woefully.

"My site will be ready to launch and, hopefully, by the end of the year I can quit my job and focus on my fitness business."

"Uh, huh." Shayla sounded far away.

"What are you thinking about?" Meg asked.

Shayla shrugged.

"Just because things didn't work out for me, doesn't mean I don't want to hear about you and Joey." Meg didn't want to be the worst best friend on the planet.

A smile spread across Shayla's face. "Since you asked, I'm super excited he's coming to visit. I'm going to show him all around Houston. Go to the zoo. Or the museum and see the mummies. Or we could go ice skating at The Galleria." She paused. "I really think I'm in love."

Meg looked at Shayla. "I want you to keep me in the loop for everything."

"I will."

"You promise?" Meg wanted to know all the details, even if it meant she'd feel a pang of regret each time.

Shayla gave her a quick glance. "Yes. I promise."

The farther away they drove from Galveston, the more Meg questioned her decision. Even if she wanted to turn around and rush back to his arms and tell him she wanted to work through things, it was too late. Drew would go back to Dallas and their momentary connection would be broken. Her head desperately tried to assure her this was still best, but her heart wasn't convinced.

CHAPTER TWENTY-ONE

Meg came home from work at the wellness center, kicked off her flats, and plopped on the couch. She grabbed her laptop and looked at her stats for her website. She'd already had two hundred visitors today and over ten thousand since her site went live over two months ago. Her Facebook ads seemed to be driving customers to her site. She had over fifty sign-ups for her subscription services, which included access to special work-outs, customized meal plans, and weekly inspirational emails. Things were starting to come together professionally.

She walked into her bedroom to change into her yoga pants and a Houston Astros t-shirt. The light glinted off the silver bracelet from Drew and caught her eye. The bracelet had sat on the far corner of her dresser because she wasn't sure what to do with it. Her head told her to toss it and forget it, but her heart couldn't quite let it go.

As she handled the bracelet, she let herself fall into a pit of memories—the walk along the street in Key West, swimming in the ocean, drinking coconut milk from an actual coconut, dancing with glow-in-the-dark jewelry, talking about dreams and about the future. Meg grasped the bracelet to her chest, wondering how Drew was doing and if he ever thought about her. She never dared ask Shayla about Drew because she wasn't prepared for the answer. Carefully, she set the bracelet back down on the dresser, then sat on the bed.

A wave of sadness washed over her. In the three months since they returned from the cruise, she'd had plenty of time to think and consider her decision to walk away from Drew. She was thrilled her online business was going well—even better than expected—but she felt hollow. There was an empty spot deep inside her. A spot that had been filled for a time by Drew.

She lay back on the bed and stared at her ceiling fan. Tonight would be no different than previous ones. Memories of middle school and the harsh words would flash through her mind and her head would try to tell her that she was better off. That she could never be happy with Drew. That she was doing the right thing. Then her heart would argue and make her remember how she felt so connected to him when they talked and laughed and danced and kissed. She absently touched her lips, the memory of his kiss still on them. Had she made the biggest mistake of her life? Had she missed out on an amazing future because she refused to let go of the past?

If she was honest, the answer was yes to both of those questions. She'd fallen for Drew and looked forward to seeing if anything would come of it. Then she'd been stunned to find out he was AJ. It was such a shock, she didn't know what to do or think or feel. She certainly wasn't the same person she was at twelve or thirteen and she'd rushed to judgment that Drew was. She let her anger make her bitter and cloud her judgment. She'd been a fool.

She wiped at a tear that edged out when her doorbell chimed. *Who can that be?* She wasn't expecting anyone. It chimed again. "Fine, I'm coming," she said, rising from her bed.

Looking through the peephole, she saw Shayla standing there. She whipped the door open and embraced her best friend.

"I'm sorry I haven't been around much." She giggled. "You know, Joey and all."

Meg pasted on a smile. "I know. Come in and sit down. We can talk. Order some pizza. Make a night of it."

Shayla stepped inside, then waved her hand. "I can't."

"Oh." Meg blinked, unsure why Shayla was there.

With a wide grin, Shayla said, "I came to get you."

"Me?"

"For dinner."

"Tonight?" She'd missed hanging out with Shayla and was tempted to go, but she was exhausted.

With excitement, Shayla said, "Yeah. Joey is in town and we want to try this new restaurant."

"Oh." Meg tensed. With Joey came the possibility of Drew. "I'm not sure—"

"Please? We want to spend some time with you. It's dinner with you, me, and Joey."

Meg let out a breath. "No one else?" She eyed Shayla suspiciously.

"No. I promise Drew won't be eating dinner with us, if that's what you're asking," Shayla said. "We haven't seen you for forever and we really want you to come."

Knowing she was beat, Meg said, "All right. I'd like to spend some time with you guys, too." She understood Shayla was in love and wanted to spend as much time with Joey as possible, but she missed having that time with her BFF. Besides, a night out might do her some good. "What time?"

"Nowish." Shayla gave her a sheepish smile.

"Can I at least change and refresh my makeup?"

"Sure. In fact, it's kind of a classy place. I brought a dress to change into." She pulled a dress from her bag. "We can get all fancy and make a night of it."

The more Meg thought about it, the more she didn't like the idea. "But I don't want to be a third wheel."

"Are you kidding? You won't be. I promise." Shayla gave Meg a hug, then said, "I've missed you and I want to spend the evening with my two most favorite people."

Meg sensed there was more to the story than Shayla was sharing. Maybe Joey was planning to propose or something tonight. Meg definitely wouldn't want to miss that. "What are we waiting for then?" She smiled.

While Shayla was fixing her hair in the bathroom, Meg rummaged through her dresses. She stopped at the blue one she'd worn on the cruise. Memories flooded her mind, making her heart hurt. She hadn't even looked at this dress since then.

"Yeah, wear that one," Shayla said as she came out of the bathroom.

"I don't know it—"

"Makes you look gorgeous."

"Thanks, but I'm not sure I want to wear this dress again." It dredged up too many feelings.

"Come on. It looks so good on you and this is a brand-new restaurant. It's going to be a-mazing." Shayla was so exuberant it was hard to deny her.

Meg couldn't remember the last time she'd gone out. She'd spent all her free time over the last couple months either working on her business or brooding over what happened with Drew. Maybe tonight she could sluff it all off and relax. "Why not?"

They chatted and laughed while Meg freshened up her make-up and brushed her hair. It had been too long since she'd spent time with Shayla. Tonight, she would go out and forget all about work, her website, the cruise, and her heartache.

"WHAT KIND of a restaurant are we going to?" Meg asked from the backseat of Joey's Lexus.

Joey and Shayla gave each other a quick glance. "Mexican," Joey said.

"No, sweetie, I think it's a vegan restaurant."

"Vegan?" Joey wrinkled his nose. "Does that mean we won't have any meat?"

Shayla laughed. "I'm kidding." She turned back to Meg. "Joey loves his meat."

Meg wasn't sure what kind of restaurant they were going to, but she was sure that Shayla and Joey were acting weird. *He must be going to propose tonight. And Shayla knows it. That's the only explanation for how they're acting.* Meg promised herself she'd play along and be the dutiful best friend. She wondered when and where they'd have the wedding.

After parking near The Galleria, they started walking along Westheimer Road. The warm mid-October evening air washed over Meg as they passed shops and other restaurants.

"It's right down here," Shayla said pointing ahead.

A small crowd gathered outside. "I wonder how long we'll have to wait," Meg said.

"Oh, we have an in," Joey said.

Shayla elbowed him. "He means we made a reservation, so we wouldn't have to wait."

A giant white banner with *Grand Opening* in black letters was strung across the front of the space. They walked past some people, then entered the restaurant. Inside, it was decorated with an Italian theme. As Meg gazed around, something gnawed at her. She attributed it to Joey's impending proposal to Shayla. Even though Meg thought they should keep dating for several more months, she was happy for her best friend.

A short woman with deep-set eyes escorted them to a booth in the back. Meg loved the ambience and the scintillating smells of oregano, garlic, and butter. "Mmm, I love Italian food."

The hostess handed them menus with a fancy handwritten font.

"I wonder what's good to eat?" Shayla said.

"Any of it," Joey said. "This Chicken Italiana looks delicious. It's the chef's special."

"I need to use the restroom," Shayla said suddenly.

"Oh, me too." Joey scooted out of the booth. Meg looked between the two of them before they hurried off. Something was definitely going on.

Meg shook her head, then studied the menu. From the corner of her eye, she saw someone approach. When she glanced up, her heart somersaulted and her stomach flip-flopped.

"Hi, Meg," Drew said.

"Uh, hi." Shayla had promised he wasn't joining them for dinner. But there he stood—looking as attractive as ever in a blue dress shirt and dark dress pants. "Shayla didn't mention you'd be eating dinner with us." She tried to keep her voice even so it wouldn't betray how her nerves were ablaze.

"May I sit down?"

She shrugged. A tapestry of emotions—shock, attraction, regret, desire, excitement, anxiety—wrapped around her.

Drew sat across from her and she struggled to not hyperventilate. It had been three months, one week, and two days since she'd seen him, but it felt like only moments ago.

"Please don't be mad at Shayla."

"You mean for setting me up? I assume this is a date or something. And they've disappeared, leaving us together." She knew Shayla wanted her to be with Drew, but she didn't think Shayla would be so overt.

"Not exactly," he said, his same musky cologne drawing her in.

Trying to keep her mind on their conversation, she said, "Then what, exactly?"

Drew smiled and Meg swallowed hard. He cleared his throat. "This is my restaurant."

She gazed at him and immediately lost her train of thought. "What?"

"I didn't think you'd come if I invited you, so I asked for Shayla's help." He leaned in and Meg's skin tingled. "I wanted you to be here for the opening."

"Why?" They'd had no contact since the cruise.

He tapped the table with his hand, then sucked in a breath. "Before I met you, this was only a daydream." He fanned out his hand. "I never thought it could be a reality. But then you came into my life on that cruise and gave me the courage to follow my dream, the way you've followed yours." He glanced down, then back at her. "I've been to your site and it inspired me to do the same thing, so I took the plunge and bought this restaurant."

"But you live in Dallas. Why did you buy a restaurant here in Houston?" It didn't make a lot of sense.

"Joey wanted to move here to be close to Shayla, and I was looking for a good opportunity. This restaurant kind of fell into my lap, and I hired Joey to be my general manager." His enthusiasm was contagious—so contagious she wanted to throw her arms around his neck and congratulate him, but she didn't.

"I hope it's successful for you," she said, still unsure how she felt about Drew. Too many feelings were colliding and swirling around her.

"Thanks."

Shayla and Joey walked back over, so Drew stood. "I have to get back to work," he said. "Enjoy your meals." With that, he left.

"Are you mad?" Shayla asked as she scooted across the booth.

"Yes. I wish you would've told me," Meg said sternly.

Shayla raised her eyebrows. "You wouldn't have come."

"But I don't like being tricked." She hadn't been prepared to see Drew again and now she was both stunned and confused. All sorts of thoughts and feelings brewed inside her.

"I know, but Drew wanted you to be here. You were his inspiration." Shayla smiled.

"I don't know about that." Meg wasn't sure she was comfortable taking credit for his decision. She didn't think she had much to do with it.

"Are you serious? The man is in love with you," Shayla said with certainty.

Meg shifted her weight and her face warmed. "No, he isn't." He couldn't still have feelings for her. Could he?

"Can we order? I'm starving," Joey said.

Shayla gave him a sharp look. "Just a minute, we're talking about Drew and Meg."

"There is no 'Drew and Meg.' And there isn't going to be," she said, not quite sure who she was trying to convince.

"Because you don't want him? Look me straight in the eye and tell me you don't think about him." Shayla stared at her. "Go ahead, tell me."

"I'm not playing this game." Meg looked directly at Shayla.

"Meg, you know I love you." Shayla clenched her fists in the air. "But you are being a complete idiot here." She let out a loud sigh.

"I'm really hungry. Like I'm about to pass out from hunger," Joey said. "Can we please order?"

"Fine." Shayla waved a waitress with short brown hair over.

After the waitress took their order, Meg snuck glances in Drew's direction. She had to admit that on the cruise, before she knew he was AJ, he'd made her feel happy, valued, content. She hadn't felt that way in a long time.

Meg watched Drew interact with the wait staff, then a customer at the front. He seemed so comfortable and genuine. He stopped at a table with a little girl wearing thick glasses who had some kind of disability. Meg guessed it was Down syndrome. He knelt near the blond-haired girl and gently took her hand in his. She grinned excitedly and he said something to her. The exchange was so tender, it made a lump form in Meg's throat. He'd grown into a gentle, kind man. A man she still cared for. Fate had thrown them together on the ship and now Fate—Shayla—had intervened again. This was her chance to make it right. To tell him what had been on her mind for the last three months. And to tell him she'd forgiven him and wanted to see what the future held.

Meg turned to Shayla. "You're right, I was an idiot."

"Huh?" Shayla perked up.

"He isn't that mean kid anymore." Meg blinked. "He's a good man."

"Yes, he is." Shayla beamed.

"When we were on the boat, I was shocked that he was AJ and my feelings were all mixed up. I was hurt all over again. And then I was mad. All that ended up doing was making me miserable." She didn't want to feel that way anymore.

"Serious?" Shayla practically jumped off her seat. "What are you going to do about it."

"I'm going to tell him."

"You are?"

"Yes. I am." Despite the blanket of fear that covered her, she was going to swallow her pride and go talk to him—something she should've done three months ago.

"Yes!" Shayla shouted.

"But what will I say? 'Hey, I was super mad at you, but you're a decent guy and maybe we can hang out sometime.'" Sounded positively stupid.

"That was the worst." Shayla crinkled her nose. "Just tell him how you really feel." Shayla encouraged her with her hands.

Summoning up all her courage, Meg rose from the table.

"We're still eating, though, right?" Joey said.

Shayla shushed him. "You've got this, Meg."

Meg's heart beat so fast she was sure it'd dive right out of her chest. With each step she took, her nerves sizzled. As she neared Drew, he was speaking to a young couple with a baby. He turned and his gaze caught hers. "Please, enjoy your dinner," he said to the couple.

"Can I talk to you?" Meg said, trying to control her quivering voice. "Privately?" No need to make this public.

"Sure." Drew seemed surprised. "We can go back to my office."

Meg followed him down a hallway willing her pulse to stop racing. Inside the office, he sat on the edge of his desk and motioned for Meg to sit in the leather padded chair.

"I'd rather stand, if you don't mind." She licked her dry lips and drummed her fingers against her thighs. "I've been thinking."

"Yes?" he laced his fingers and set them in his lap.

Being in such close proximity to Drew and trying to corral her thoughts was too much. Her head shouted at her to run while she had the chance. She turned toward the door. "I'm sorry I can't—"

Before she could take another step, Drew was next to her, his hands on her trembling arms. "Please, tell me what you came to say."

"Well, I . . . I . . ." Where should she begin? Her heart told her to just trust in herself and her feelings.

"Meg, I'm so sorry for all the things I said to you when we were kids." He peered at her.

"I know you are." She paused, listening to her heart. "On the ship, when I met you, I felt a strong connection and I let myself fall for you." She swallowed hard. "I was stunned when I realized you were AJ. After the shock wore off, I was angry and hurt all over again. I wasn't thinking clearly." She paused. "I've had the chance to think about it over the last three months and I've realized some things."

Drew studied her. "Such as?"

"You've long since left AJ behind, but I hadn't. All the memories of that time kept playing over and over in my head. I wanted to keep reminding you and punishing you, so that I'd feel better."

"Did you?" he asked softly.

"Nope." She shook her head. "Just made myself completely miserable. But now I see . . ."

"What?"

She straightened. "I see a good man with a kind heart. A man . . ."

"Yes?" he said anxiously.

Meg took a deep breath. "A man I can see a future with." There she'd said it and she couldn't call it back. Even if he felt differently, at least she'd said her piece.

Drew didn't say anything for a few moments. Her heartbeat thundered in her ears while she anticipated his response.

Finally, he said, "You're sure?"

Biting her lip, she nodded. She was sure. Very sure.

He moved in closer and brushed a tendril of hair from her face, then traced his finger along the outline of her ear. Goosebumps erupted across her shoulders and down her back.

"I haven't stopped thinking about you. So many times, I wanted to call or go over and see you, but I was afraid you'd refuse because you were still mad. But I couldn't get you out of my head."

"The past is the past, and it needs to stay there. I know that now." She didn't want to be stuck in the past anymore, she wanted to move forward.

He smiled, then wrapped his arms around her and she melted into his embrace, every part of her clinging to him. They stood there, intertwined, for a minute or so as she reveled in the strength of his arms and how naturally they seemed to fit together.

He moved his head slightly away from hers and gazed deeply into her eyes. Slowly, his hand cupped her chin. His mouth hovered over hers, making her want—no—making her yearn for this long-awaited kiss. Gently, he laid his warm lips across hers and gave her a tentative kiss. He pulled back and gazed at her again, his eyes asking for permission. She leaned into him, every cell in her body on alert, and kissed him. This time, the kiss was confident and strong—their mouths giving and taking. She couldn't imagine doing anything else except kissing him for the rest of her life.

After he pulled back, she gulped for some air.

"Wow," he said. "Even better than I remember."

She gave a smile that reached from the tip of her head to the bottom of her feet. Finally, her heart and head agreed.

"I have a confession," he whispered as he rested his forehead against hers.

"Oh, yeah?"

"I've moved in with Joey. I got a job with a law firm downtown and I'll be working there until this restaurant takes off."

She pulled back enough to gaze at him. "You don't live in Dallas anymore?"

"Nope." He grinned and the skin around his eyes crinkled. "I live here."

"That's the best news I've heard in a long time."

"No," he said, tracing her jawline and letting his finger trail down her neck. "The best news is that we're together. I can't wait to see what the future holds."

CHAPTER TWENTY-TWO

Meg stood on deck, gazing out over the ocean. Moonbeams bounced across the vast, open water and the warm, salty air washed over her. Drew snuggled up behind her, his strong arms embracing her. It was a perfect moment out in the middle of the sea.

"I can't believe all that's happened over the last year," Meg said. "Shayla and Joey getting married and buying a house, you becoming a full-time restaurant owner and part-time chef, my online business growing. So much has happened."

"And?" he said, nuzzling her neck.

"That's a pretty amazing year, wouldn't you say." She turned around and faced him with a smile.

"What was the most amazing part?" He played with a lock of her hair.

"Hmmm. Let me think about it," she teased.

"Think about it?" He pulled her close and tickled her until she squealed.

Laughing, she said, "I have to admit, there were some other

pretty amazing things too. Like the first time you told me you loved me." The memory sent a flicker of delight coursing through her.

"I remember," he said, his whole face radiating love. "I was so nervous."

"Why?"

"Because I wanted to wait until I was sure you felt the same way, but I couldn't. I just knew I loved you, so I blurted it out at the grocery store, of all places." He shook his head. "I didn't even know if you'd say it back."

"But I did. Right there in the soup aisle." Meg caressed his cheek and he leaned into her palm and kissed it.

"Yes, you did." He embraced her.

They stood there, wrapped in each other's arms for several moments, Meg taking it all in. She'd never thought she could be so happy, so content.

"Anything else amazing happen?" he asked.

She pulled back. "Well, there was this pretty awesome proposal that included dozens of roses and a late-night candlelight dinner in this highly-rated Italian restaurant near The Galleria."

"That turned out pretty well." He gave her a proud grin. "Shayla helped me a little, but most of it was me." He patted his chest proudly.

Meg grasped his hands in hers. "Then our wedding day last week. Everything about it was exactly how I'd imagined it." Meg recalled the day and pure bliss enveloped her. "And coming on a cruise was the perfect honeymoon idea."

"It's where it all began," he said.

"It is."

Drew looked deeply into her eyes, making her breathe faster. "I meant what I said last week. I will spend my life loving you and doing all I can to make you happy."

"I know." She squeezed his hands. "And I will do the same."

He gave her a tender kiss, leaving no doubt he was all hers. "We should come on a cruise every year to celebrate," he said.

"That's a fantastic idea. Except. . ."

"What?" He studied her.

Not quite sure how to put it, but knowing she wanted one more thing to make their life together complete, she said, "Maybe next year we can add an extra passenger?"

He lifted an eyebrow, then smiled. With a nod, he said, "Happy to oblige."

ABOUT THE AUTHOR

Rebecca Talley grew up next to the ocean in Santa Barbara, California. She spent her youth at the beach collecting seashells and building sandcastles. She graduated from high school and left for college, where she met and married her sweetheart, Del.

Del and Rebecca are the sometimes frazzled, but always grateful, parents of ten wildly- creative and multi-talented children and the grandparents of the most adorable grandkids in the universe.

After spending nineteen years in rural Colorado with horses, cows, sheep, goats, rabbits, and donkeys, Rebecca and her family moved to a suburb of Houston, Texas, where she spends most of her time in the pool trying to avoid the heat and humidity. When she isn't in the pool, she loves to date her husband, play with her kids and grandkids, swim in the ocean, eat Dove dark chocolate, and dance to disco music while she cleans the house.

You can join her Reader News to keep up with her crazy life, including her new releases, and receive your complimentary ebook, *Best Kind of Love*, at www.rebeccatalley.com.

BOOKS BY REBECCA TALLEY

- ROAD TO ROMANCE
- IMPERFECT LOVE
- SPEAK TO MY HEART
- WEDDING WEEKEND
- ADDING CHRISTMAS

BOOKS IN THIS SERIES

- BEST KIND OF LOVE
- FLIPPING FOR LOVE
- ON DECK FOR LOVE

POST A REVIEW

Please consider leaving a review on Amazon. If you have an Amazon account, you can go to the book description page and write a review for this novel. Authors love reviews!!

Reviews help authors find new readers and help readers find new authors.

Thank you!

FREE Download

Will Brynn recognize the
best kind of love when she sees it?

Best Kind of Love: A Reunion Romance Novella Kindle Edition
by Rebecca Talley (Author)
98 customer reviews

amazonkindle

"This was a fantastic story!"
Gina K.

"The chemistry between the characters is great..."
Karen G.

When you join
Rebecca Talley's Reader News
you'll receive a complimentary copy
in your preferred ebook format.

Go to her website www.rebeccatalley.com and join today!

Made in the USA
Columbia, SC
19 December 2024

50070268R00102